THE MEMORY
OF AN ELEPHANT

THE MEMORY
OF AN ELEPHANT

A Novel

by

Alex Lasker

Please visit my website at

www.alexlasker.com

Dedicated to Dame Daphne Sheldrick
of the David Sheldrick Wildlife Trust

and

All the caretakers and all the rangers
fighting to save the African elephant

CONTENTS

PROLOGUE

HAD IT NOT BEEN for the torrential rains, the events of that night and beyond might have turned out very differently. But because the visibility was barely fifty meters, and because the wipers of his Mercedes were too taxed to clear the windshield properly, Dr. Ovidio Salazar was traveling only forty mph on a highway designated for seventy-five.

A giant shape suddenly appeared in Salazar's headlights and he swerved instinctively, which sent his car into a tailspin, which he corrected—wrongly—by braking and turning away from the spin, which magnified the result into a sliding, full-on 360. When the car finally came to rest—without slamming into the median barrier or the creature, thankfully—Salazar looked out to see what the hell the beast had been.

And there, standing not twenty feet from his windshield, was the biggest elephant he had ever seen. It was staring in at him through the wipers with what Salazar would later tell his family was concern, he was sure of it. Their eyes locked for a good five seconds, and then the elephant turned and easily stepped over the median barrier, quickly disappearing under the curtain of rain. Had there been any other traffic, the elephant would have created more havoc, or even been struck, but as it was well before dawn, only people like the doctor, who had to be in a surgical O.R. in Lusaka in an hour, were on the road.

What was an elephant doing on a highway in the first place? Salazar asked himself as he pulled to the side of the highway to let his heart slow enough to drive again. There weren't any national parks for hundreds of miles, there was no "trail" leading through the suburban developments and townships that spanned north from Lusaka, so this creature was either a runaway from a zoo—highly unlikely, since Salazar didn't know of any—

or he was an escapee from a national park and had somehow traversed the outskirts of civilization for hundreds of miles without being noticed.

Until now.

* * *

I know that I am coming to the end of my days. The pain in my body slows me, the hunger for a good meal taunts me, and my eyes grow cloudier and dimmer by the day. I've seen this before many times, and I know what the end will bring. So my journey back to the place where I was born, to the ones who cared for me, if they are still there, is all that is left for me. The distance and the exact direction are unknown to me, but I have no doubt that my senses will tell me where to go. I just hope to get there in time.

I remember every sight, every sound, every smell from the moment of my birth to the moment we are in now. I have no dates to mark the time by, and no knowledge of the two-leggers' boundaries, but I know I've been far from my home, taken to distant lands and climates, across endless waters to towering nests filled with noise and unbearably bright lights where countless of them hurtle about in their false beasts.

My world is out under the open sky, where the stars are so close you can see them moving across the night. Where the only thing you hear is the thrum of insects, the roar of predators carried on the breeze, or the screeching of the tree dwellers—and the dread silence of those who have to sleep on the ground.

It is under that sky that I hope to end my journey, among the two-legged friends who raised me, and the friends from my long ago adopted herd, the wonderful aunts and cousins who took me in as if they were all my mothers.

* * *

Trevor Blackmon, the 53-year old assistant game warden for Zambia's national parks, hung up the phone and scowled. This was going to be a headache. If the sighting was bona fide—and the witness was a surgeon, so he was probably reliable—how had such a large animal been able to avoid detection in a fairly populated area for the several days it would have taken it to travel from the nearest national park?

Now Blackmon was going to have to locate the elephant, probably from the air, and dispatch it before it caused any major problems—like trampling some innocent family in their back yard—and before the beast came to the attention of the animal activists. They would demand that it be tranquilized and transported back to a park, which, with a fifteen-thousand pound bull—and this surely had to be a bull, females rarely traveled alone—would be the biggest headache of all. It would be far easier and more convenient to wait until it was in a tribal area, far from prying eyes, dispatch it and let nature take its course with the corpse. There were 25,000 elephants in Zambia, after all, one less bull wasn't going to be a concern.

First, Blackmon would check the satellite tracking office for any GPS devices that might be transmitting, and if he was lucky and the bull had been fitted with a collar, or had had a chip implanted, it would make locating him a snap. Blackmon knew this was a long shot, since no alarms had gone off yet, but that might be explained by the budget cuts that had gutted the staff whose duties included monitoring the devices. But it was worth a shot, so he picked up the phone again and stared out at the downpour as he waited for the call to go through.

—Zambia, Present Day (The Long Rains of 2012)

CHAPTER ONE

First Memories—Kenya, 1962

UNLIKE YOU, WE REMEMBER *our first hours. I believe you have little memory of your lives until you are able to walk. Not us. We walk on our very first day or risk being eaten by predators. I hovered under the massive shadow of my mother, tripping and stumbling blindly, stuffing my face up into her belly to suck the sweet milk dripping from her breasts.*

Sounds and smells overwhelmed me: the grasses and the soil under foot, the boom of thunder and the loud patter of the afternoon rain, the fat brown river and its slippery banks, the strange horned animals drinking at the watering hole with us, the pungent smell of the herd's urine and dung. There were too many members in my clan for me to count, but I recall my sisters and brothers and aunts welcoming me in those first days with a profusion of trunks, stroking and encouraging me, letting me know each of them by their scent.

My mother's patient wisdom guided me through learning the rules of survival, her shape and scent always close by, never leaving me behind when I dawdled or grew tired. The hours stolen with my playmates—there were six of us calves—were the antidote to the many worries. I'd fall asleep, aching with wonderful pains, and then be up with the sun to do it all over again.

Other than my herd mates, my best friend was a young buck of the Shaggy Beard variety. They have the strange habit of suddenly leaping and spinning in the air and pounding their heads against imaginary trees. My mother finally told me why; they are born with maggots in their heads, and when they grow older the maggots hatch and try to find a way out, which drives the poor beasts crazy.

Though it is not common for elephants to fraternize with other species, my mother allowed us to play every day while our two herds spent a rainy season at a sprawling river complex. My friend wouldn't listen to his mother,

5

who tried in vain to keep him from joining us, but then she'd leave him, understanding that our herd would watch over him if he was with me. We would wander off and explore for hours, butting and smelling everything, from animal holes to dung to insects, until one of us would get hungry and we'd go nurse from our mothers.

It eventually dawned on me that everything we did was watched over by my herd's adult females, and then I was confronted with the horrible reason why. We are always a moment away from some terrible, blood-freezing danger, no matter our size or age. The best defense we have is numbers: stay with the herd, and the chances of being taken are slim. Walk alone, and your days are numbered. But even numbers can sometimes let you down.

My Shaggy Beard friend was drinking at the riverbank with the rest of his herd when a flash of motion leapt from the water and grabbed him. It was a Big Snapper, and she dragged him under until all we could see were his legs kicking desperately above the surface. I screamed to his herd to do something, but none of them would move. They just stared, paralyzed, and I heard their minds as clear as if they could speak (which they can't): They were glad it was him and not them.

They trotted away when several other Big Snappers joined in, and the river burst with their violent tails and the water turned red. The sounds of my friend's last helpless grunts still haunt me. It was a shock to my heart, and to this day I have never been that carefree again.

Our first rule was to always be aware of the big cats and the sloped dogs lurking in the grass, their cold eyes watching everything. But the most terrifying creatures of all were you, you two-leggers. Not those who would appear in their foul-smelling false beasts and watch us from a distance, shiny little objects clutched to their faces, clicking and whirring. Nor the tribes-people we passed on our travels who lived in nests of dried mud and sticks, who tolerated us as long as we stayed away from their fenced crops.

No, the two-leggers who scared us most were the ones who would steal downwind of us to get as close as possible without us scenting them. The tall, black-skinned fast runners who would surprise us with their sharp sticks. If you were pricked, it would mean a slow, painful death over hours or even days. The young hunters were the worst of them; they seemed to take pleasure in causing a needless death.

But the most dangerous of all were the white-skinned hunters, because they could kill from a great distance. Their false beast's noise would fall silent somewhere far off, and we would raise our trunks and try to scent where they might be. Soon the birds would fall silent and dread would fill the air. Then would come the echo of one of their boom sticks and one of our adults would stagger. We would thunder away as soon as we saw them, but it was already too late. You could see the stunned look in the victim's eyes, and then he would crash to the ground in a cloud of death. Hours later we would return to find the ravaged corpse. They would hack off the tusks and trunk and leave the body bleeding and faceless, and we would cry and call to our departed friend far into the night.

Every season we would return to the places where our friends had fallen and visit their bones, turning them over and over, remembering their owner, and hoping to find a life force in there somewhere. But it was always gone.

* * *

My mother, called Moon Mother by our clan, became the leader of the herd during the rainy season of my second year. Red Eye, our beloved matriarch, could barely eat because her teeth were gone, and her voice hardly registered. I say "voice" knowing you do not understand our language, nor can you even hear it; it is far too low for your ears. But we have conversations just as you do, sometimes over long distances, like our brethren in the sea. Their sounds carry through water, ours through the air or the earth. At night we can address relatives many horizons away; if we stand three-legged on hard ground, we can hear other families sending messages from half a day's walk away—through our feet.

When Red Eye finally collapsed and could not rise again, the herd stayed with her for two days and nights, each of us reciting our fondest memories of our time with her. On the third day she stared at the rising sun with her beautiful eyes—she was known for her long lashes and her one red eye—and her sadness gave way to acceptance. Then, as we all wept, she left us.

We were lost until a new matriarch was anointed. Red Eye held the stored wisdom of sixty rainy seasons and knew, for instance, every watering hole and underground aquifer hidden among hundreds of miles of savanna and highland. In the dry season, that knowledge could be crucial to our survival.

I was too young to understand what happened next, but recognize now why the mood of the herd was so disturbed, and why I had such troubled, violent dreams: There was a war of succession going on between my mother and another older female, She Storms. You may not perceive different personalities in us, but we are each just as unique in our world as you are in yours. And just as you have your troubled among you, so do we.

She Storms was crazy, and had been since she'd been struck by lightning in her youth. But she had survived and had a large extended family, of which she was the eldest, and therefore their leader. Now she had started a subtle war with my mother, determined that she would become the new matriarch, even though most of the herd favored my mother.

Then She Storms did something unthinkable. She had been quietly threatening me for days—when my mother wasn't looking—and as we crossed a rain-swollen river, all the adults, my mother included, were concerned with a dangerous current that was swallowing the younger calves for several seconds before they could find their footing again and finish crossing. She Storms, who was bringing up the rear and had let all the other calves pass her but me, suddenly pinned me with her tusks and held me under in water deep enough that no one could see me. She was twenty times my size, and I couldn't do a thing; I was unable to even get my trunk above the surface. I screamed desperately with the last breath I had left, hoping that some relative would hear me. Then I started inhaling water.

Sensing something, my mother turned and looked for me, then realized what was happening. As she charged through the water, She Storms let go and I surfaced, gasping. I watched as my mother, enraged, gored She Storms so severely that she fell and was swept downriver before she could clamber onto the bank. She limped out of the water, screeching with pain, and then everyone saw that she was bleeding profusely.

"What have you done, Moon Mother?" screamed She Storms' sister as their clan gathered around her, all of them trumpeting and snorting and gaping at her wounds. "She could die of these!"

Our family surrounded me and my mother protectively, and then my mother finally spoke.

"She was trying to drown my little one, I saw her with my own eyes. Ask him, he will tell you."

She Storms wailed, "Don't listen to her! I did no such thing! She's mad!"

"Let the little one speak," bellowed Crackles, an older cow who was not from either of our families, so her opinion on this matter would be respected. "Speak up, Moon Mother's son." They all looked down at me. But I was so shaken, still retching up water, that I couldn't find my voice.

A strange look came over my mother, and she spoke to the gathering in dawning comprehension. "She was thinking...that I would be so broken-hearted by my son's death...that she would become our matriarch! She was plotting to take over our clan by drowning my baby, do you see?"

She Storms' family let out a chorus of stomping and trumpeting, and She Storms kept on denying it.

"Oh no, oh no, she's making this all up! I love that little calf like my own son!" That she treated her own son far from lovingly was not mentioned.

Crackles bent over me, inserted her trunk in my mouth and whispered, "You must tell them what you saw, little one, or this could be very bad for your mother. Tell the herd what happened."

I have always been a sensitive male—even in later years as a grown bull—and it pained me to accuse her, even after what she had done. But now she had lied, and even though she could kill me with one blow from her feet, I had to speak up. I looked around, seeing clearly for the first time, and noticed that all the horned animals on the banks were watching us in silent awe.

My voice was weak and small. I recounted the events as best I could, saw the stunned looks in the herd's eyes, then finished by defending my mother's actions.

"So you see, she had no choice but to use her tusks." I lowered my head. "That is the truth. That is what happened."

Even as She Storms continued to protest, now calling me a liar, the rest of the herd looked at one another in consternation. She had gone too far this time. Crackles called for a meeting of the elder cows. As my mother and She Storms were kept apart, surrounded by their families, the elder cows somberly walked into a stand of trees and began to speak, their voices rumbling quietly.

Some of my sisters and aunts tried to patch things up between the two families, but too much damage had been done. Family is the key to survival in the wild, and even though her behavior had been deranged, She Storms was her family's leader, and they had to stand with her.

A few minutes later the elders returned. Crackles cleared her throat and addressed the herd solemnly.

"We have come to a regrettable, but unavoidable, conclusion. After countless seasons together, after many lost relatives and friends, we will no longer be able to travel with She Storms. After what she did here today, to a helpless calf born of one of our most respected elders, we cannot trust her to be in our presence again. She is hereby banished from this clan. If they so wish, any members of her family can travel with us, but they are free to go with their matriarch. That is our ruling."

She Storms's family was probably not surprised, but there was a lot of upset over the ruling, and then they had to decide whether to stay with the herd or go with their family. In the end, they all went with their matriarch, for good or ill, and a little while later they left us. As a lone bull I crossed paths with them over the years, but, sadly, it was never the same, even with my former calf friends.

Now my mother would lead the rest of us, making all the important decisions, like when to rest in the heat, when to climb into the highlands for dry season, when to seek safety, or attack, if danger approached. The females had all watched and learned from Red Eye, and now they would watch and learn from my mother. One never knew when they might be called upon to lead or to throw up their bodies as a protective wall. And the females ruled everything, from the raising of calves to the cold banishing, at adolescence, of all young bulls.

I may have boasted a bit about the accuracy of my memory, because there is a blank spot in my early years that I cannot account for. There is a Before—me with my wonderful mother, my doting brothers and sisters, and the rest of the herd all living in a lush valley during rainy season—and an After, when I awoke on a farm in the highlands among two-leggers I had never seen before.

They had stolen me away from my world and my family, and I was helpless to do anything. I am ashamed to say that all I did was cry and thrash about, but my heart was aching so badly that I had no other response. They were forcing a strange-smelling liquid down my throat as they held me. There were none of my kind to be found, though there were other plains-dwellers, all *young like me. I was in a waking dream; my memory of that time is so foggy that I have no idea how long it was or what had happened to me.*

And after that, everything in my life was changed forever.

CHAPTER TWO

Other Voices—Kenya, 1964

THE POACHERS CAME ON horseback at dawn, a method their leader had attempted by himself a week earlier to see if it would work. It had been so successful that he was riding among the herd as if he were invisible. The great beasts had thought his steed was just another creature of the plains. The rider was ignored for several minutes until his scent finally spooked them and they took off.

So now the herd they had tracked for a day was grazing peacefully in a lush meadow, most of them out in the open, not paying any attention to the riders as they dismounted, one by one, every twenty meters inside the far tree line and unslung their rifles. A morning mist was just lifting; the sounds of the elephants' trunks snapping branches off mopane trees echoed like gunshots.

The matriarch looked up, sensing something wrong, then picked up their scent before she saw them. She swung her mighty form head-on towards the far tree line and trumpeted a warning. The females quickly gathered in a semi-circle, shielding the calves and infants behind them.

Then the matriarch spotted the lead poacher as he stepped out from behind a tree, his skin as black as night, his eyes as impenetrable as a cobra's. She flared her great ears out and charged, hoping to scare him. But he stood his ground, raised his .375 H&H rifle and calmly squeezed the trigger.

The bullet entered her skull directly above the trunk and mushroomed through her brain before it exited into her spinal cavity. She dropped head first, the earth shaking from the impact of her massive weight. Then the other rifles opened up and the herd wheeled in panic. They had never encountered this kind of killing before; they were too stunned to react, their leader was lying in a heap, this was way beyond anything they could comprehend.

There were thirty-two of them with tusks big enough to take. They called to each other in desperation as they fell, family to family, intoning final farewells over the rifles' constant firing. In less than two minutes they were all dead or dying, and the men moved out from the trees and walked among them, finishing off those who were dragging themselves to lay beside their loved ones, flailing their trunks and weeping, with shots into their ear canals.

The calves that were too small to shoot huddled a short distance away, bewildered. The infants—there were six of them, two years old at the most—stood by their mothers, puddles of urine at their feet, their eyes wide with terror.

The poachers pulled machetes or axes from their saddles and set about their business. The lives of these animals meant only one thing to these men, and that was money. They started hacking away at the elephants' faces, cutting deep into the flesh around the tusks so they could carve them out whole.

When the lead poacher reached the matriarch and began hacking away, he felt something poke at his back and whirled. The matriarch's calf was wheezing at him in distress with his tiny trunk. The poacher slashed his machete across the elephant's forehead, and the creature wailed in pain and trundled away a few yards, blood seeping down into his eyes.

The poacher finished hacking off the tusks and was about to toss them into the pile when the baby approached him again—but this time charged. The poacher dropped the tusks, gripped his machete with both hands, and thrust the blade deep into the calf's forehead. The little elephant made not a sound…and collapsed against his mother's carcass.

* * *

Fourteen-year old Kamau Matiba had spent the night in the crook of a baobob tree, and he had not slept well. He'd dabbed the ointment his mother had given him on the wounded site every few hours, but it still burned badly. He'd gritted his teeth and shown no reaction when they cut his foreskin off in the ancient rite of Kikuyu manhood, because that was expected. But now, alone out here in the dark miles from his village, it hurt something fierce.

He'd climbed back down at dawn after eating a strip of dried springbok, tied his robe tightly and hefted his spear. He would have to stay in the bush for three more days on his own, and when he returned he would officially be a man. Kamau was highly intelligent, so this struck him as a bit ridiculous, but he understood the culture of his elders, even if they harked back to another century and wanted to remain there. Kamau did not, and with Kenya's recently-won independence from the British, which he'd learned all about in his village's school, he had big plans for how he was going to leave village life behind soon enough. But for now, he had to play along.

He'd been walking for a while when, somewhere in the far distance, he heard the gunshots. Dozens of them, as if there was a war going on over the hills. After almost two minutes they stopped, and there was a deathly silence. He knew he should avoid going anywhere near that place.

Then, a while later, he saw the dark specks floating in the sky. Circling. He figured the distance to the site as three or four kilometers; there were no roads in this area of the park, so whoever had been firing probably came on foot. He jogged up the hill until he could see down to the next valley, just to be sure. He certainly didn't want to run into them.

Even if he'd had binoculars, whatever had been shot was not visible through the stands of riverine trees. He was about to head back down the hill when he felt the earth vibrating under his feet, and then felt the air move from the thudding of hooves. He turned and stared, trying to ascertain where the animals were coming from. It dawned on him that they were coming from the valley where the killings had occurred—and he ducked into a wall of brush just as the first horse galloped into view.

Kamau stole deeper into the cover and watched. He had a clear view as the riders galloped past not fifty meters away. There were six of them, all with rifles, and they had extra horses with heavy, bloodstained canvas packs bouncing against their flanks.

When they'd disappeared he stepped cautiously back into the open. He could see them down below now, heading west. They wore non-tribal

garb—shorts, T-shirts, sandals or tennis shoes, floppy hats or ballcaps—
so he couldn't tell what tribe they were from, but there were only a few
possibilities. And they'd likely be from somewhere within a thirty to for-
ty-kilometer radius, which narrowed the choices even more.

He turned back toward the killing field, his nerves on edge, but his
curiosity stronger. He set off at a gentle lope.

Kamau came upon the meadow from the tree line and froze in his
tracks. The ground was saturated with blood, urine and dung that had
escaped the creatures in their death spasms. Their lifeless eyes stared out
as if the last image they had beheld was seared into their retinas. Kamau
wasn't prepared for the level of atrocity he now faced, and he had to fight
the urge to vomit.

He walked out and started chasing the vultures off, but they just
hopped down a row and started ripping at flesh from another carved-up
face. All the tusks had been hacked off the huge corpses except for five
infant calves, shot in the head for no reason he could see but cruelty.

Kamau's insides were roiling, his throat could hardly swallow. He
heard a weak whiffing issue from nearby; it wasn't the birds, it was something else. He stepped over a puddle of entrails, slapping at the vultures
with his spear, and came upon the saddest sight of all. A sixth calf, lying
next to its mother with a machete blade sticking out of its forehead, the
handle broken off.

He knelt down and touched the poor creature—and then recoiled in
surprise. It had opened its eyes and was staring at him. Kamau jumped
to his feet.

"Little one, you are *alive?!*"

The little elephant tried to get to his feet. Kamau clicked soothingly
and tried to hold him down so the machete wouldn't do more damage,
but the young elephant calf weighed 500 pounds, so there wasn't much
he could do. Once it was on its feet, Kamau stared into its eyes head-on
and saw the dull, desperate look of shock and pain. Kamau couldn't contain himself, and tears ran down his cheeks in anguish. At that moment
he was ashamed to be human.

The elephant stared at him, his breathing labored, his trunk hanging listlessly, for several seconds, understanding, on some level, that this

gentle human was different than the cobra-eyed one who had hurt him. Then he looked down at his mother's body, slowly sank to his knees, and lay down beside her again.

Kamau whispered to him, "You stay here by your mother, little *tembo*. I'll be back with someone who can help you, okay? I'll be back as fast as I can."

He whirled and chased after the encroaching vultures, yelling and waving angrily, scattering them momentarily. Then he took off at a run.

Chapter Three

Salisbury Hill Farm—Kenya, 1964

THE RAMBLING OLD COMPOUND sat on a rise overlooking its farm acres as well as a panorama of Tsavo West National Park beyond it for fifty kilometers in every direction. Other than goats and chickens for milk and eggs, no farm animals were allowed, since they would attract any carnivore that passed downwind of them, and the crops were meager at best—every passing herd of herbivores, from elephants to dik-diks, had a go at them—but the family didn't seem to mind. That was probably because the current residents were a professional white hunter and his family.

Russell Hathaway had been raised in London and gone to college at Oxford until the war interrupted. After spending two years in the Eighth Army in North Africa, he realized his calling was out under the open sky, not in a corporate office in London, and when he took a trip to East Africa on leave, he saw his future laid out like a treasure map unfurling on a lantern-lit table. Now, at thirty-eight, he guided safaris for the biggest outfit in East Africa, Lord & Stanley Ltd., and he was as happy as he would ever be. The feeling may have been short-lived, but he didn't expect any different. As a young officer he'd seen how life could change everything around you in an instant. His strapping physique and blond, wholesome looks were catnip for his clients' wives, but in a way that didn't threaten their husbands' egos, which were outsized—they were among the richest, most powerful men in the world. European royalty, corporate chieftains, Hollywood icons, families of great inherited wealth.

His wife Jean was in Nairobi at the moment with their twelve-year old son Terence, shopping for clothes for his first year away at an English boarding school. Jean tried to hide her beauty by wearing virtually no makeup and tying her cascade of blonde hair in a low, loose ponytail, but it had almost the opposite effect. No one who met her wasn't dazed or charmed.

She ran the compound, which was staffed by half a dozen "boys"—as all black males, be they six or sixty, were then called—who cooked, cleaned, and attended to the family as well as the farm, and serviced the myriad vehicles and supplies needed to stay in the wild for weeks at a time. While Lord & Stanley booked clients from around the world, pulling permits, arranging flights and pickups, bribing the necessary civil servants to keep the lucrative business going, Jean did the bookkeeping and bill-paying for the hundred or so "boys" who would show up from their villages and townships when the message went out that a safari was imminent.

But her true love was a small orphanage she ran on the grounds. The word for hundreds of miles around was that she would take in any abandoned infant animal, try to nurse it back to health, and if it survived, return it to the wild. This was a nascent period in animal rescue, before most current methods were tried and perfected, and a majority of the infants—especially elephants—died of shock, heartbreak, or lack of the proper nursing formula. But she was undaunted, and with each grieving over an innocent's death, she swore she would find the formula for keeping them alive. Much like she'd seen the world changed with the advent of antibiotics twenty years before, she was going to persist until she discovered it.

Russell was working under the hood of one of his Land Rovers when Nyaga, his forty-year old major domo, came into the four-car garage and summoned him with some whispered words of an emergency in the park twenty kilometers to the south. A young Kikuyu had run all the way to tell them. Russell wiped his hands on a rag and quickly went with Nyaga.

This caught the attention of his fourteen-year old daughter Amanda, a tomboyish redhead who was home from her Nairobi boarding school for a long weekend. She set her book down—she was reading the new bestseller, Harper Lee's "To Kill a Mockingbird"—and quietly followed.

Russell was shown to Kamau, seated in the shade just outside the kitchen door, bathed in sweat and drinking water while speaking in Swahili with Russell's two Waliangulu gun-bearers. Russell smiled at the solemn-eyed, graceful Kikuyu and offered his hand. Kamau rose from his squatting position respectfully and, his eyes averted, shook Russell's hand—or rather, held his hand limply and allowed it to be shaken. This European hand-shaking custom was something the locals tolerated with equal parts awkwardness and resolution.

Russell began speaking in Kikuyu.

"My name is Russell Hathaway, Kamau. I hear you ran all the way from the Ngulia area. Thank you for coming so far, my wife and I really appreciate it. Where exactly did you see these elephants?"

The boy answered, not in Kikuyu, but in perfect English.

"In a meadow just by the river, where the first hills begin before the highlands. I will show you."

Russell stared open-mouthed, the gun-bearers traded startled glances, and Amanda grinned, which for her was rare since her teeth were a tangled mess of braces. Russell finally asked, "Where the hell did you learn to speak such lovely English?"

Kamau shrugged, but he was holding in a smile.

"We have a teacher who comes to our village school from time to time. Mrs. Fitzgerald is her name. She is British."

"I must meet her one of these days. She sounds impressive."

Kamau just nodded, but he found himself already liking this white man; his aura was warm and his deep blue eyes appeared to take everything in, and he seemed not to possess the superior attitude of most Europeans living in the colonies.

"Well," Russell continued, "we should get moving and see if we can save this poor creature." With that he rattled off several commands to the gun bearers, who escorted Kamau out to the garage as Russell hurried into the main house and unlocked the gun cabinet.

"Daddy," Amanda said behind him, "since Mum and Terry aren't here, I'd better come along. It's the only prudent thing to do. Besides, you need a female to talk to the little elephant."

She was so sure of herself it made Russell smile, but he knew better than to expose her to such carnage.

"There's going to be a lot of blood. Your mother would be quite upset if I took you along."

"She'll be fine with it. After all, I've dug lots of graves and seen lots of bloody injuries. You can't shelter me forever."

Russell chambered several rounds in his Weatherby and locked the cabinet. She was a lot like he was at this age; he couldn't grow up fast enough either. He sighed, recognizing that to not take her would make him a hypocrite, something he hated in others.

"OK, climb in the back. But if you get sick, don't come crying on my shoulder."

* * *

The little elephant was dreaming. In his dream it was getting dark and he was famished, but he was having the hardest time trying to find his mother to slake his hunger. Every time he spotted her in the gloaming she moved away, and he couldn't run fast enough to catch up to her. His head throbbed with pain.

Suddenly a new pain gripped him, this one coming from his left hind leg. In the dream it hobbled him and he cried out to his mother, but her huge form just melted into the shadows. He screamed, thrashing helplessly as she disappeared.

He awoke in blinding daylight and the pain was even worse. He raised his head and saw an incomprehensible sight: a slope-dog was tearing at his left leg, its snout wet with blood. The little elephant kicked reflexively and the hyena went flying head-over-heels. It got up again and shook its head, dull-eyed and nasty. The elephant scrambled to its feet and, listing badly, stared the hyena down. Several vultures, who were gorging on his mother nearby, hissed to each other and watched with interest.

A popping noise suddenly rent the air and the little elephant's head whirled. It was one of his aunties; her stomach, swelling with gases under the hot sun, had burst open. Blood and entrails poured out, and the birds and slope dogs leaped toward the hot, gushing meal.

* * *

The rescue party took two vehicles, a Land Rover and one of the safari trucks that had a hydraulic lift. Russell had Kamau sitting in front with him in the Land Rover as they sped south on the park's unpaved road, then left the road at Kamau's direction. Now there was just window-high grass and an occasional stand of acacias. Russell had a second sense about driving off-road, which was a required skill: hit an unexpected rock or hole going 50 mph and your axle and suspension would be shot. Worse, you'd end up with a spine or head injury. Seat belts were just appearing in cars, and no one would start using them for several years.

Six kilometers in, Kamau pointed to a distant line of trees and a green belt, where Russell knew the river ran. Soon enough Russell steered toward the vortex below a thousand-foot-high gyre of vultures. The vehicles scared off a pair of hyenas who were heading toward the site, and pretty soon they were in the meadow.

As Russell got a look at the carnage he turned to his daughter behind him.

"Stay in the car until we make sure it's safe." He knew it was safe, but wanted to shield his daughter from the sight of it.

A dozen hyenas' bloody snouts and crazed eyes glared at the intruders as Russell and Kamau, Nyaga, and the two Waliangulu gun-bearers stepped from the vehicles. Russell raised his Weatherby and fired into the air, the ear-splitting report causing the vultures to screech and take off in a maelstrom of wings. Yips of protest went up from the hyenas, but they too turned and trotted into the trees to watch.

The men stood and stared, all of them sickened, but Russell was more angered. He looked at the older of the two gun-bearers, Kagwe, who was a hunter and tracker of great renown, and nodded at the shell casings littering the ground.

"When we're done here, take Mathu and see if you can find out who did this." The buzzing of flies was so loud he had to raise his voice to be heard.

Kamau spotted the little elephant standing beside its mother, trying to suckle from her, and whispered soothingly, "There you are, little friend. I told you I'd be back…"

Russell joined him and saw the machete blade protruding from the calf's forehead and cursed under his breath. In fact it was a quiet torrent of profanity, and if the poachers could have seen him, they might not have slept so well after drinking themselves into oblivion that night.

Russell realized Amanda was standing behind him, her eyes brimming with tears. He felt guilty that he'd brought her now—she had obviously not expected anything like this—but she needed to see the savagery men were capable of. Years later she would tell him that this day was the most formative incident of her young life, that everything she did afterward was influenced by this searing memory. She thanked him for it, even though it changed her feelings about humanity forever.

The elephant looked up at the humans with a confusing mixture of emotions. They were clearly the kind that had obliterated his family just hours before, and some of them were carrying the same oily, metallic-smelling devices that had done the killing. But there was something reassuring in their behavior that settled him somewhat, and the smallest of them, an orange-crowned creature with a young female scent, knelt down beside him with a bowl of strange-smelling white liquid. He was so deliriously hungry by now that he sniffed at it with desperate interest, but he couldn't get his trunk to work.

Amanda tried to stop crying as she whispered to the little calf, holding the mixture of cream and goat's milk under its limp, listless trunk.

"Oh, Daddy, he can't even drink..."

"Some of the muscles must have been severed. He won't make it through the night if we don't get him back to the farm."

Russell took out the syringe he'd packed in the medical kit and stood behind the elephant. He jabbed the needle into its hind quarters and pressed the tranquilizer in. The elephant shifted slightly, but otherwise he had no reaction for a moment. Then he wheezed softly, slowly crumpled to his knees and flopped onto his side.

* * *

As Nyaga backed the safari truck up to the farm's rear outbuilding, a menagerie of orphaned animals gathered at the fence and watched the lift lowering the new arrival. Russell had injected the antidote to the tranquilizer as soon as they'd secured the calf in his enclosure, and now, as the metal cage reached the ground, his blindfold was taken off and the door was flung open.

The elephant blinked and looked around through the fog in his head and the toxic smell of diesel exhaust. The sight of human habitation alarmed him—all elephant calves were taught to avoid these places, they could mean death in an instant—so his heart rate went up several notches. He also didn't understand the contraption he was in, so it came as a rude surprise when he was pulled forward by a rope and pushed from the rear—and then he was out. Neither did he realize that there had been a blade impaled in his forehead—it had entered in the blind spot between his eyes—so he didn't realize that Russell had removed it and temporarily bandaged the wound, as well as the laceration across his forehead. The pain in his head was not quite as intense now.

With Kamau stroking him gently, Russell, Amanda and two keepers led the elephant into a roofed enclosure separate from the other animals and covered him with a thick woolen blanket. The highlands are cool and damp in rainy season, and young calves could die from virtually any change to their systems without their mothers feeding and warming them.

"I'm going to radio my wife," said Russell as he turned to go. "Kamau, if you could stay here and look after our boy until she arrives, that would be super."

"Yes, Mr. Russell," Kamau said as he knelt beside the little elephant, whose eyes peered out at his strange new surroundings from behind several already soiled, drooping bandages.

* * *

Russell and Amanda drove to the airstrip to pick up Jean and Terence, who had flown from Nairobi on one of Lord & Stanley's bush planes the moment they'd gotten the radio call. Terence was the spitting image of his father—beneath a twelve-year old boy's typical layer of fat and an awkwardness that, even though he was a straight A student, reduced him to monosyllabic responses or pained silence.

Jean had attempted to save several orphaned elephants in the past. Each time they'd lived for a week or two, but they weren't getting enough nourishment with any of the animal milks she'd tried. Each time one of the little creatures died, everyone on the farm was bereft. But those orphans had all been less than a year old, when mother's milk is crucial to survival. This one was thought to be almost two, so there was a chance. And this time she was going to mix coconut oil with human baby formula to try to match the fat content of elephant milk.

* * *

The four family members walked straight from the Land Rover to the enclosure, where Kamau rose quickly from beside the now-sleeping calf. Dusk was falling, so several hanging kerosene lanterns had been lit.

"Darling, this is the young man I was telling you about," whispered Russell. "Kamau, meet Mrs. Hathaway…and my son Terence."

Kamau looked down shyly as they each offered their hands to shake.

"It's a pleasure to meet you, Kamau," said Jean softly. "My husband is a tough judge of character, and he already thinks you're quite extraordinary."

"I thank you, Miss Jean. I have heard about you and this place since I was very young, and I am so happy to make your acquaintance."

Jean was instantly charmed. He struck her as wise beyond his years, not a hunter, but a thinker. And one with a big heart. Terence didn't say anything, but he watched Kamau with quiet fascination.

"Well, let's see our new charge," Jean said and knelt beside the little elephant. He looked forlorn under his blanket and bandages, and Jean muttered under her breath, "Bloody bastards."

Then she got a look at his long, heartbreaking eyelashes and was completely smitten. "I'm going to go brew some formula for our little friend here," she whispered to Kamau as she rose, "and then you're going to feed him the first bottle."

Jean walked in twenty minutes later with three bottles and handed one to Kamau.

"Just lift his trunk and slip it into his mouth. He'll do the rest."

Kamau cooed softly into the orphan's ear, lifted his trunk and slipped the bottle in. The calf didn't understand at first, until Kamau tipped the bottle and the formula trickled out. Then the elephant sucked at the nipple hungrily, and to their delight the formula was gone in seconds.

The second bottle, which Amanda fed him, had the same result. Then Terence took a turn, and a light seemed to come on in the little elephant's eyes.

Well, Jean thought, at least he liked the taste, and he knew he needed nourishment.

* * *

Hillary Cole, Tsavo West's doctor and veterinarian, had driven over from the park's main gate forty kilometers to the south. Leathery and ropy under an unruly mane of white hair, he was infamous for his flinty bedside manner. Russell led him into the enclosure now, where he knelt beside the little elephant, carefully removed the bandages and examined the wound with a head-mounted light. The calf recoiled as Cole probed the wound.

"His sinus has been ruptured," Cole finally said as he stood up. "From the amount of bacteria he's been exposed to, you're looking at a major infection." He pulled a syringe from his kit, filled it with penicillin—the biggest gun of that time—and injected the elephant's rump.

"It's been what, twelve hours?" he asked Russell and Jean.

"His herd was wiped out just after dawn," said Russell upon looking at Kamau, who nodded.

"Then you can expect a raging fever later tonight," said the vet. He pulled out two more ampules and handed them to Jean. "If his symptoms don't improve within six hours of onset, give him another dose." He closed up his bag and snapped off his gloves.

"What are his chances?" asked Jean, who clearly picked up on Cole's guarded prognosis.

"It all depends on how strong he is," Cole answered as he regarded the little creature. "How strong his will to live is. You'll know by tomorrow."

That evening after dinner Russell was called to the radio room. There was rather urgent news; one of Lord & Stanley's other hunters had had an accident on a safari in Masai Mara and they needed someone to fill in for the last week. Russell would have to catch a bush plane in the morning.

Russell visited Kamau and the orphan in the shed to say his good-byes. He had already asked Kamau to stay on for a few days to see to the orphan's transition—at least until Kamau was due back in his village—but now Russell had an offer to make.

"Kamau, Mrs. Hathaway and I have been talking. We feel you're a most exceptional young man. If you want it, there's a job for you here in the orphanage. You'll have to leave your village for the time being, but I gather from my trackers you're not so keen on staying there for the rest of your life, eh?"

Kamau's answer was a crooked smile.

"We'll take care of your schooling. Hell, we'll pay Mrs. Fitzgerald to come out whenever you like. Just stay with us here through public school, and we'll see where things go."

Kamau stared back at Russell, struggling to find words.

"I would like…very much to think about it. To speak with my family. It is a very kind offer of you."

"Fair enough." Russell held out his hand and Kamau put his out limply. "Kamau, make your hand firm like mine. And look me in the eye. You're going to be shaking a lot of hands from now on, might as well learn properly."

Kamau strengthened his grip and his eyes crept up cautiously to meet Russell's, who smiled.

"Brilliant. I hope to see you in a week's time, then. Good luck with your charge. Oh, and it would be fitting if you came up with a name for him, eh? You saved his life, after all." And with that Russell turned and was gone.

The fever swept over the calf late that night like a hurricane, wiping out what little energy he'd had and causing him to tremble as if he were freezing, yet his temperature was now up to 103. Cole had schooled them on how to hydrate him and bring down his temperature, and it took three caregivers at a time. He needed to be sponged constantly with tepid water, and even if he refused, he had to be forced to drink fluids.

By midnight delirium overtook him, and he became dangerous to his keepers in the enclosed stall. A 500-pound animal could easily crush a human's ribs or a leg by shifting unexpectedly, so Kamau, Jean and Nyaga took turns sitting with him on his straw bedding, warily keeping him company. Elephant calves will not sleep without an adult figure nearby— even human, if that's all there is—and they'll look up constantly to make sure someone is with them. The longing in a young elephant's eyes is haunting, and the attachment between the two species quickly becomes profound, sometimes even more so for the humans.

At three a.m., as rain poured down outside, his fever reached a perilous 105 and the delirium became acute. Jean injected another dose of penicillin and called to him desperately as he lay there. Jean didn't say it to the others, but she thought they were going to lose him. His eyes were fixed on somewhere far from this place; he thrashed and wheezed and his sinus ran with a mixture of infected mucous and blood. There were moments in the delirium where his keepers could see he was there with them and aware of his surroundings, and then the storm would slam into him again and he'd be gone, his body twitching, his legs pumping in a fever dream.

Jean hardly slept in the nearby cot, and except for her labors giving birth to her children, and a night spent in an Underground tunnel during the Blitz, this was the longest, most trying night she'd ever endured.

The fever broke just before dawn, and at first Jean thought he was dead, he was so still. Then she realized his eyes were watching her.

"Hello there, little one," she said softly. "How are we feeling?"

As she crouched down, his trunk curled up toward her and touched her face. At that she couldn't contain herself and she dissolved into tears. She took a reading—101—and laid her head on his, letting her tears stream down onto his sweet, wrinkled brown face. He exhaled loudly through his trunk and raised his head, looking around as if seeing her, and this leaky shed, for the first time.

CHAPTER FOUR

Salisbury Hill Farm and Eldama Ravine, 1964

I MUST HAVE FALLEN DOWN *a mountainside, I remember thinking as I awoke; I was so stiff and sore, nothing else could explain it. My head felt like I'd been gored by an angry Long-Horned Snout. Years later I came to know one of them in my travels—he was in the pen across from mine where I first saw snow—and not only is it true they are nearly blind, they're also preternaturally dull. I could never carry on a conversation with him, even though we were both stuck there for what would presumably be the rest of our lives. The tree-dwellers in the higher cages were better conversationalists, I must say, if a bit loud.*

As I slowly wobbled around my new surroundings I had the feeling that there was a major piece of my life missing. And then, as the fog in my head gradually lifted, it occurred to me: where was my clan? What had happened to my mother, my family? There was no sign of them. The other animals were simple-minded plains dwellers, so they could shed no light on what this place was or why we were there. We all had the nice two-leggers feeding and looking after us, but it's disconcerting to be snatched from your loved ones and wake up alone with no explanation.

The young two-legger who shadowed me and fed me the strange new milk was certainly no substitute for my mother, but there was something kind and familiar about him. As I tested the landscape for my mother's scent, up and down the hillside following the high barrier fence that blocked my way, I started to become cross. A young shaggy-beard like my old playmate kept butting me from behind, until I finally turned and knocked him down.

That set all the two-leggers to running, so I started running too. Tail straight back, trunk straight out, feet moving fast, as is our youthful way. I

31

crashed into the barrier and collapsed in anguish and fresh pain, and then got
really woozy and fell back asleep.

Kamau hadn't mentioned it to anyone, least of all anyone at Salisbury
Farm, but he'd had an uneasy feeling about the poachers he'd witnessed
riding away that day. The one on the lead horse, anyway. The man's face
had seemed vaguely familiar, but galloping by, seen through undergrowth,
Kamau couldn't be sure. Or at least that's what he'd convinced himself of.
But the memory gnawed at him and wouldn't go away.

Kamau had returned to his village three days after helping save the
elephant calf and, after putting his younger brothers and sisters to sleep,
went in to bid his parents goodnight. In a speech he'd been rehearsing
in his head for days, he told them what had happened on his walkabout,
and of the white hunter's offer. They were as surprised and suspicious
as he thought they might be, and demanded to meet the family before
talking any further.

But they were also proud and, eventually, slightly larcenous about
the opportunity. He would be able to send back a nice portion of his pay,
wouldn't he? And he would be properly educated; in time he would be
able to find a good job in the city, perhaps even work in the new government. They saw the possibilities cascading ahead over the years, at least
as far as two village-raised parents could, and began, if a bit nervously, to
embrace them.

Then, a day before Russell was to return from Masai Mara—Kamau
was going to arrive at the farm that morning to begin work in the
orphanage—the poacher's identity came to him as he woke from a fitful,
dream-filled sleep.

Kamau had been about eight years old. He remembered him from
their village. If it was the same man, he had been about seventeen at the
time, and he'd been a bully who Kamau and all his friends were afraid of.
He would never remember Kamau, because he'd never paid any attention
to younger boys. Then, Kamau remembered, he'd beaten an older boy
so badly—over a perceived insult—that the victim's parents had sworn a
revenge oath and several family members had come looking for him late
that night. He'd had to flee the village, and had not been seen since.

His face had changed somewhat since he'd matured, but as Kamau ran the scene of the riders over and over again in his mind, he realized that this man was one and the same. His name had been Gichinga Kimathi, and in the last six years he'd apparently become even more cruel.

* * *

The township of Eldama Ravine was typical of most rural outposts springing up throughout the East African countryside at the time. An industrious landowner had set up a little *duka*, or store, beside a red dirt road carved below a series of lush hills in 1959. Like a seed, that *duka* had spread and transformed, over a few years, into a way station for more than 3,000 tribes-people who wanted to leave village life behind, but didn't have the stake or the daring to make it all the way to Nairobi, a hundred miles away. There, the shantytowns were like a hellish version of Dicken's London, where you could disappear and either become an African Fagin, or—far more likely—never be heard from again.

The townships were made of scrap, plywood and tin, had no running water or electricity, and occasionally washed away in a heavy rain, but they offered a new kind of life for those who wanted out of the 15th century. Quickly there followed alcohol and prostitution, then piles of garbage and junked cars in the muddy alleyways, raw sewage and disease, and a thriving criminal underworld.

It was into Eldama Ravine under a wet, thundering sky that Kagwe and Mathu walked two days after Russell had sent them on their mission to track down the poachers. They'd followed the trail of the horses from the meadow to the main road and found the tire tracks of a truck that had met them and ostensibly taken on the ivory. Following tire tracks on a well-traveled dirt road is a fool's errand, so they'd followed the horses, all the way out of the park and eventually to this township some thirty kilometers to the northwest. Horses were a rarity in Kenya—due to the bite of the tsetse fly, whose sleeping sickness would infect them within days—so they assumed the horses had been destined for meat, and been "borrowed" for a few days by the poachers before being slaughtered.

Kagwe found a Luo butcher's establishment while Mathu located a mechanic working out of his front yard, and before long each had leads on who might have had an interest in horses and who might have big bore rifles for a good price. Then they'd reconnoitered and found that their leads were both Kikuyu and located in the same part of the township. When they found the shacks, they saw that they shared a common wall, the same tin roof and a newly-constructed wooden porch, which for a township like Eldama Ravine indicated the occupants had some means.

Being great trackers and bow hunters, Kagwe and Mathu possessed a skill few people appreciate, and that is the art of disappearing into one's surroundings so completely that no human, or animal, is aware that they are there…until it's way too late. An hour later they were rewarded by the two occupants' return, and as they observed the men's behavior, they were drawn to the leaner of the two: his cold black eyes and demeaning treatment of his companion told them all they needed to know.

As the two men drank palm whiskey and played cards while the rain peppered down on their tin roof, the trackers had little doubt that the lean one was the brains behind the operation, that his temper was violent, and that he seemed dangerously ambitious. They'd learned that his name was, appropriately, Gichinga. The "Firebrand."

* * *

The Beechcraft Baron taxied to a stop by the waiting Land Rover in a cloud of dust and prop wash and Russell clambered out into the evening's cool. His first question to Jean, after jumping into the car's passenger seat and kissing her on the mouth—they still had an elemental attraction to each other after fifteen years of marriage and two children—was how the elephant was doing.

"Not only has he survived," she answered, "he's taken over the orphanage with his charm. Humans and animals alike. He definitely likes getting his way, even if it takes throwing his weight around."

"Is that going to be a problem?"

"No, no, he learns really quickly. He's a smart one."

"How's our young Kikuyu?"

"He's taken to the job as if he was born to it." Jean mused for a moment as she drove. "I have the definite impression he'll end up running the place one day."

"Let's not get ahead of ourselves. He's been here less than a week."

Another Land Rover—this one older and painted camouflage—was approaching from the opposite direction. Both drivers blinked their headlights and pulled to a stop in the middle of the road, window to window.

Ian Masterson, a bearded sixty-year old who looked more like a college professor than the game warden for Tsavo, poked his head out.

"Doc told me about your new orphan. How's he faring?"

"He's healing up nicely and drinking the formula like an old hand," answered Jean. "We think he's got a good chance."

"Excellent." Masterson looked past Jean to Russell. "What about Terence, isn't he leaving for England soon?"

"In the morning, in fact," Russell answered. "Ian, you missed your calling as a town gossip."

Masterson laughed. "Minding other people's business is my way of staying young and vital."

"We'll miss him come weekends," said Jean with a sigh. "But at least he'll have my parents close by in Staffordshire."

Terence had been attending an all-boys boarding school in Nairobi, but now he had a spot waiting for him at The Bedford School north of London, just as there had been a spot for Russell and six generations of Hathaway men before him. In the British system, upper class sons were expected to go away to school at age eight or nine, and they did so without complaint.

"Hang on a moment," said Masterson as he climbed out of his Land Rover and fished a burlap bag and a snake pole from the back. A thick, ten-foot long cobra was slithering across the road. Masterson expertly scooped it up, dropped it in the bag, cinched it and then set the squirming sack in the rear seat.

At that moment a family of giraffes strode majestically past the two vehicles, not twenty meters away. As accustomed as the three humans were to seeing animals every day of their lives, they all watched in silent wonder.

After dinner Russell visited the keepers, who were just getting their charges to bed. Kamau was in the shed with the elephant, reading by a hanging lamp as Russell walked in.

"So glad to hear you can stay with us. Are your parents OK with everything? Do we need to drop by and put on a little show for them?"

Kamau had jumped to his feet, his big eyes smiling, and shook his head.

"That will not be necessary, Mr. Russell. They are pleased for me, and the good things this job may bring. I thank you for the opportunity again, and hope I can live up to it."

"I have no doubt you'll do fine." Russell knelt down and stroked the calf, who was lying on his side watching them both. He examined the wound and the stitches in his forehead. "I see he's healing nicely. Do we have a name for him yet?"

"I think so, Mr. Russell. 'Anaishi.' I hope you approve."

Russell thought for a moment, then nodded. "Excellent. Very fitting. 'He lives...he remains...' They couldn't kill him, eh?" Russell looked down at the calf with a smile. "Would you permit "Ishi" for a shortened version? Easier to call him in a hurry, eh?"

Kamau beamed and looked to the floor.

"I was thinking that as well, yes. Ishi." He repeated it softly to the elephant, whose ear flapped open and closed.

Russell drove Jean and Terence to the airstrip in the morning to see them off. As Jean stepped onto the wing and ducked inside into a seat behind the pilot, Russell held his son close and whispered in his ear.

"There may be times when you feel so lonely you'll think you're living on the dark side of the moon. When you feel like that, remember, I went through it too. So did my father, and his father before him. It's completely natural. You just have to get through it." He hugged his son and stroked his cheek gently. "Remember how much we love you and try to stay strong, because if you let the older boys see you showing weakness, they'll make your life miserable. Do you hear what I'm saying?"

Terence nodded. He tried his best to give his dad a last smile, then climbed aboard the old twin Beechcraft. Russell squeezed his shoulder one last time, nodded to his wife, and then closed the door.

The props quickly coughed to life and the plane turned and taxied away. Russell held his arm aloft as the Baron raced by and jumped into the air.

Jean would be back from Nairobi tonight, so Russell had a day to himself. A day he would use to go hunting—but not for game.

He had gone out to the staff's quarters late the night before and found Kagwe and Mathu by the fire. As he smoked his pipe they told him of their journey to Eldama Ravine and what they had found, and now the three of them, with a little help from Ian Masterson, were going to pay this Gichinga a visit. They had no verifiable proof of anything yet, but Russell was confident enough that he had called a high-placed friend in the local constabulary and had him request a warrant from the Attorney General's office in Nairobi. It would do for now.

Russell thought about what it meant to these poachers, and the feeling made him uneasy. Here he was guiding rich white men to a mature bull, then standing by as they shot the life out of it and had the tusks shipped home to mount for their vanity. He was paid good money for this. Except for the $5,000 paid for the license to shoot an elephant—$50,000 in today's currency, money that would go to the care of other animals in the park—was there a difference in killing elephants for their ivory if you were a poor African? Was this not a bit hypocritical?

And Kagwe and Mathu had been well-known poachers in their day, as were many gun bearers in the safari trade. The Waliangulu were fierce hunters who used poison-tipped arrows to bring down bull elephants, but they hunted as a tribal ritual and for meat, not to sell ivory to crooked middle men for the Asian black market. They had been hunting for centuries, well before the white man arrived and "educated" them that killing elephants was not in their best interests. In Kagwe and Mathu's cases, they had finally been caught and convicted by the authorities, served their sentences, and were now "rehabilitated."

But in any case, the cruelty of the slaughter Russell had witnessed the week prior was different. The wanton destruction of an entire herd with high-powered rifles made Russell realize he had to come down harder on this Gichinga than the usual garden variety poacher. Or he would be back for more.

* * *

The three of them drove to Eldama Ravine and met Ian Masterson and two of his trackers standing beside his Land Rover. All of them were armed, their rifles visible to keep anyone who had possible ideas at a healthy distance.

Mathu went with Masterson's group, who parked at the rear of the township and approached the shacks from an alley behind them. Russell and Kagwe walked in from the road out front and, when the second hand on Russell's watch struck 11:15:00, they stepped onto the porch.

A young woman with a baby in her arms stared out at them as they filled the screen door, Kagwe's rifle cocked and leveled, Russell's Weatherby held loosely in one hand.

"I'd like to have a word with your husband, please," Russell began in Kikuyu. "Have him come out here on the porch and no one will get hurt."

There was a sharp noise from the rear, a door or window slamming open, and then several voices shouting in Kikuyu.

"Stop! Get down!"

Masterson and Mathu had stepped out of the shadows at the rear and cut the would-be fugitive off, guns aimed directly at his head. Mathu recognized the young man as he fell to his knees, pleading for them not to shoot. Mathu called to the front.

"Mr. Russell, it's the other one! Gichinga's still inside!"

The woman in front of Russell stood frozen, her eyes wide. The baby started to squall. Russell raised his voice, but added no alarm to it.

"Gichinga, I just want a word with you. Please come out onto the porch and no one will get hurt."

A moment later a figure emerged from the bedroom, hands aloft. He was dressed only in a T-shirt and shorts, his lean arms knotted with decorative scars. Kagwe nodded that this was Gichinga, and Russell motioned for him to come outside. He could feel the eyes of scores of residents watching them from the shacks nearby.

Gichinga ordered his wife to take the baby into the bedroom and shut the door, then stepped outside and met Russell's eyes without even a hint of fear. He sat down on the step and calmly lit a cigarette. Russell stayed standing, but lowered his Weatherby.

"I assume you know why we're here," Russell resumed in Kikuyu. "Your horses' tracks led us from the Ngulia area almost to your door. I and the warden are the keepers of Tsavo National Park, and it is an affront to us, or to any civilized person, to have someone slaughter protected animals in our park. Especially the way you did."

"Your park?" Gichinga scoffed, then spit onto the dirt. "I was under the impression there had been a change in the government. The parks are now owned by the people of Kenya, not the British."

Russell kept his expression neutral, but he had to restrain himself from knocking this bastard's teeth out with his rifle stock.

"Nothing's changed as far as the law goes. Poaching is a crime under the new government's laws just like the old ones, punishable by prison and fines. And where did you get this insolent attitude? Who the hell do you think you are?"

"I think I'm not so much insolent as I am…confident. Confident that the ways of your world are not going to be with us much longer. That we will be able to have jobs and make money like you have been making off our land for years. Maybe if there were jobs like that now, my people wouldn't be forced to kill your sacred animals for money, eh?"

"You're dead wrong there. And they're your animals as much as they're ours. The sooner you people realize that, the better."

The men from the rear detail appeared now with Gichinga's cohort, whose hands were tied behind his back. Masterson joined Russell and looked coolly at Gichinga. Russell continued.

"But none of your talk deals with the reason we're here today. You and your friends are guilty of murdering an entire herd of elephants and leaving them to rot in the sun. I assume this was someone else's idea, so I'd like to know whose. Who paid you to do this? Who bought the tusks?"

Gichinga dragged deeply on his cigarette, then slowly let it out through his nostrils. "And if I were to tell you, you wouldn't take us away and whip us until we bleed?" He said it with a disingenuous smile.

"Because if you think we're still living in that time, you are wrong, old man."

Russell glanced at Masterson, whose reaction to Gichinga was even more shocked than his. This man was shrewd and dangerous. He was obviously not some simple-minded poacher; he was going to be a force to be reckoned with down the road.

"I've never hit a man for poaching," Russell answered. "Or whipped one. That doesn't happen on my watch." He leaned close to Gichinga so only the two of them and Masterson could hear. "Now, I've shot at one or two, I'll admit it, but they were just warning shots. I wouldn't miss if I tried. If I heard about something happening in my park again like what happened last week, I'd kill every last one of them, let *them* rot in the sun. Am I clear?"

Gichinga nodded, then tossed his cigarette down on the dirt and, to the dismay of the two white men, crushed it out with his bare foot.

"But I must warn you as well," he answered. "The kind of person you are interested in finding might be very powerful. So powerful, you should stay far away. You could lose your license and be forced to leave our country if you pursue this. Am *I* clear?"

Russell stood back and stared, his anger replaced by something cold and as yet unformed. He realized what it was. He was seeing the future—of his life, of his family's, of the British people's—in East Africa. This man was the first wave of a future that was going to change everything Russell had known here.

All he could say was, "We'll see about that. But in the meantime, I'm going to offer you a deal. You can either give us the name of your buyer…and walk free…or you're coming with us to Nairobi. The Magistrate is waiting for us there with charges brought by the Attorney General's Office, and that's going to mean you and your friend here will spend the next several years in prison." Russell looked back inside Gichinga's darkened rooms. "Be a real hardship on your wife and baby, I'd think. But it's completely up to you."

Gichinga sighed heavily, but it was mostly because this was going to ruin his plans to drink and play mahjong with some friends that afternoon. He rose and put his arms out in front of him to be handcuffed.

"Go ahead then, let's play out your game. Let's all take a drive to Nairobi."

Russell tried not to show his temper, but it got the best of him. He nodded to Mathu, who produced a length of twine, and then Russell spun Gichinga around and yanked his arms behind him. Mathu quickly tied his wrists, whereupon Russell pulled the knot as tight as possible to make sure it hurt.

"You have any clothes you'd rather wear? They'll provide you with a uniform in the jail, but you might want to make a better impression on the Magistrate."

Gichinga just smiled and shook his head, as if he didn't have a care in the world. As they led him and his partner away, Gichinga looked back and called to his wife.

"Tell the boys we'll be home for dinner by tomorrow night."

CHAPTER FIVE

Zambia, Present Day

THE RAIN HAD FINALLY stopped as Trevor Blackmon parked by the side of the T2 highway and stepped from his Toyota Land Cruiser. A mist hung from the forest canopy as vehicles thundered by behind him, their wakes rocking his car. He rubbed at the still-painful site of his latest ink—a python, the insignia of his old unit in the Rhodesian Army, coiled on his heavily-muscled forearm—and walked for a ways, peering through the undergrowth at the highway's protective cyclone fence until he found it.

The trampled foliage in front of it was a dead giveaway: the fence had been cut through, probably by locals who wanted to cross the highway without walking several miles to reach the next overpass. The hole had rusted and widened over time and finally collapsed until it was a gaping invitation. The autos hurtling by at 80 mph would never notice the breach.

He walked further in, looking down at the muddy puddles of rainwater, then stopped.

"Mother*fuck*," he muttered. He knelt down; an elephant's unmistakable tracks led from the hole in the fence toward the concrete highway. So the doctor hadn't been hallucinating.

This was most definitely a large bull on the move. If he had escaped from a park, it would almost assuredly have been from Lower Zambezi, but why would he be heading north? Through civilization? The area he had already crossed was mostly commercial farms and communal lands; there was a corridor for wildlife built in, but this bull had gone off the reservation some seventy miles back, according to the map on Blackmon's Droid, and now he had wandered across a highway and was heading for populated areas.

If he was healthy, why would he leave the sanctuary of a protected park, where there was vegetation, water, and females over a ten-thousand square mile expanse—everything a mature bull would need? Did this mean he was *not* healthy? Was he a danger now? It certainly seemed to add up to that, which meant that they would have to deal with him even sooner than Blackmon had first surmised.

He peered at the map, scrolling northward toward the next city, Kabwe. They had maybe two days before the bull reached its outskirts. If Blackmon didn't hear back from the GPS people by this afternoon—or if their satellite showed no evidence of a chip or a collar roaming in the area—Blackmon would have to bring in a tracker. And fast.

* * *

The night is my friend. It has always been so. Though my eyes aren't what they once were, I can see enough, and my sense of smell is still quite sharp. So I travel in the dark, quietly on my soft feet, passing the lights of the occasional two-legger nest in the distance. I can smell and hear them coming for miles, and I know to give them a wide berth. Occasionally one of their domesticated beasts will follow me for a while, barking its hollow threats, but I just move on, and they eventually give up and return to their beds.

I lay up in the trees during the day and eat what grasses are available— my teeth cannot chew bark or leaves anymore, so I don't even bother with them—and I sleep on my side if the shade is right, and my old form is not visible to any passersby. I can cover maybe half the distance I could have in my prime, but age has taught me to save my energy and to stay out of sight of the two-leggers. Even though some of them can be kind and helpful, you never know which one might be your undoing. The world we travel in is circumscribed by theirs, I realized that long ago. They are the rulers of this earth, there are too many of them, and the rest of us are at their mercy.

CHAPTER SIX

Salisbury Hill Farm—Kenya, 1964

THE PLACE WHERE I WAS raised was filled with kind and helpful two-leggers, and I have fond memories of my time there. Once I got used to the idea that I was no longer part of a herd, that I had no mother or relatives to watch over me, that I was not allowed to escape the hilltop except in the company of my caregivers—things became more bearable.

The dark-skinned male who first discovered me was my constant companion, and we would spar and play for hours on end. The matriarch of their family became my mother in a way; her discipline and cross tone when I would act badly was something I tried to avoid at all costs. They and the sweet, orange-crowned female would provide me with rich, tasty milk from a hidden mother somewhere, though I never met her.

The male of their family was a great source of interest to me; since I had no males of my own to learn from, I watched his behavior closely whenever he came around. Every other two-legger would defer to him even though he didn't demand it—it was just something that hung about him like a scent. Even I was drawn in by his deep, all-seeing eyes; it gave me a warm, dizzy feeling when he would whisper to me, face to face, as he roughly stroked my temples.

One still, moonlit night I was awakened by a distant sound that made my heart leap with recognition. My two-legger companion sleeping beside me did not stir, and I realized that he could not hear it, even though it rumbled like thunder inside me. It was my kind! They were passing somewhere below the hilltop, and two of them were having a noisy argument. I could hear the rest of the herd by their footsteps, but they weren't joining in the fight.

I quickly got to my feet and ran out to the fence, and now I could scent them as well as hear the other members conversing quietly. I cried out as loudly as I could, and they all fell silent. Then I spoke—in a way I didn't even *know I knew—in a voice that I had never used. I asked them who they were, and if they knew anything of a family whose matriarch was named Moon Mother.*

I heard them talk quietly among themselves, and then the matriarch's voice rumbled back a response.

"Kindly don't shriek, young one. Who are you, and what are you doing here with the two-leggers?" Her attitude was not friendly or welcoming; in fact she reminded me of She Storms.

At that moment my two-legged companion appeared beside me, addressing me in concerned tones, and tried to lead me back to my bed. I pulled away from him and trotted up to the highest point of the hilltop fence, and then I could see them in the distance, outlined by the brightness of the moon.

They were looking up the hill at me, and then my companion arrived and saw them too. He clicked and whispered approvingly, and I answered the matriarch.

"I was too young to be named when I lost my herd, and now I live with the two-leggers here. Have you any knowledge of my old clan? Maybe you have heard of some of them—One Tusk, Always Sleepy, Hears Nothing…?"

There was a quiet, intense conversation among the herd—it went on longer than I was comfortable with—and then the matriarch responded.

"We have some members of our herd who knew your kin, little one. They don't have good news for you, I fear." I dreaded to hear her words, but they came anyway.

"Your family was slaughtered by two-leggers sometime during the last rainy season. Their bodies were found by the clan of She Who Kills Lions, and when they had been reduced to bones, they were buried beside the river where they fell. But if you were from this family, how did you not know of this?"

Kamau heard the grieving noise that emitted from Ishi and mistook it for a desire to escape the compound and join the herd. He could not have known that the little elephant was overcome by heartbreak. Then the squealing noise gave way to a disturbing wheezing in his throat. He wheeled and ran down the hill and threw himself into the "watering hole"—a pond they had dug with a tractor a while back—and immersed himself until only his trunk could be seen.

Kamau stood by the watering hole, at a loss, and then Mama Jean was there beside them, wondering what the commotion was all about. Kamau began to explain what he'd seen—when Ishi emerged from the water, his body language so sunken that he appeared to be crushed by an invisible weight. Then Jean looked up and squeezed Kamau's arm as she indicated the barrier fence beyond them. Two of the passing herd's females stood there, not ten meters from them. Even though Ishi would not look at the elephants, Jean and Kamau could tell there was some sort of communication going on between them.

"Little One, you will have to grieve for your family now. We are very sorry for your loss. I am told your mother was a well-loved matriarch."

I was so overwhelmed with the news of my family's fate that I couldn't speak. After a moment the second female spoke; she had the kindest voice I'd ever heard.

"You are too young to travel with us yet, Little One, but we will be back this way again after each rainy season. When you are ready to join us, we will wait at the bottom of the hill, and maybe your two-legged friends will let you go. They are said to be quite kind."

I think I might have mumbled something in gratitude—because this speaker was so wise and gentle—and then wandered back to my bed. I was freezing cold from the water, but more, my heart was freezing cold from the shock. My two-legged companions brought warm milk and draped blankets over me and then stayed with me for the rest of the night while I shook.

And so it was that Ishi began to change. He grew up faster from that day on, as if, now that he knew how he had come to be an orphan, he was planning for his eventual departure from Salisbury Farm. And he would have to be stronger and more mature in order for a non-familial herd to accept him, he knew this instinctively.

He weaned himself from the milk formula and began eating only vegetation. He stopped playing with the other orphaned animals as much, though he still had a soft spot for a young zebra calf who shadowed him everywhere and slept beside him most nights. It was no longer as easy for Kamau or the other keepers to coax him into their daily sparring matches or games of hide and seek, which Jean had instituted to emulate the games he would have played with his siblings in the wild.

His daily walks outside the farm began to get longer and longer; Ishi would test his keepers' patience as he strayed further and further out into the hills. Finally, one afternoon's walk turned into evening and, when he refused to turn back as darkness fell, one of the keepers ran back to Salisbury to fetch Russell. Russell pulled his Land Rover up in front of Ishi, blocking his way, then jumped out and stood in front of the headlights, his face inches from Ishi's.

"You're here by our good graces, and I'll be damned if you're going to get away with this bloody nonsense. Now get yourself back to the farm right this instant."

Ishi stared at Russell, and though he didn't understand the words yet—that would come many years later—he understood Russell's tone and his outstretched arm, pointing back to Salisbury over the hills. Looking hurt—his trunk drooping, his eyes downcast—he turned and started walking back the way he'd come, and when his keepers started jogging, he picked up his pace and ran ahead of them, all the way home.

* * *

Two weeks after his confrontation with the poachers, Russell found himself in Mombasa on business for Lord & Stanley. While there, he decided to call on an old friend from the former colonial government, Rupert Matthews, who had been Kenya's Finance Minister until independence and was now one of the owners of the two most prestigious hotels in Kenya, The New Stanley in Nairobi and The Crown in Mombasa. He was extremely well-connected, and Russell figured he'd know about the higher-echelon players in the ivory trade since Mombasa, Kenya's port city, was the main trans-shipment point for all goods, legal and illegal, that entered or exited the country.

It had been a painful realization for Russell when, the day after they'd had Gichinga Kimathi arrested and charged, he received a radio call from Ian Masterson, who was spitting mad.

"They bloody well walked out this morning. Free as you please."

"Who?" Russell had asked, perplexed.

"Your damned poachers, that's who. Some newly-minted attorney from the Interior Ministry showed up and set the two of them free. Said the charges were based on flimsy evidence and there won't even be a fine! He just let them walk out!"

Russell had felt his face flush with humiliation. It was hard to swallow, but the bastard had gotten the better of him, that was now clear. And he'd even predicted the outcome. So the game was rigged, and now Russell would have to take the law into his own hands if he was to prevent more wholesale butchery. Well, so be it. He'd shot men before, though it had always been at a distance—and in a war. He realized that this too was a kind of war, and that he could do it again, here in his adopted land. He would just have to be very careful about it.

Russell and Rupert Matthews sat at the Crown Hotel's pool bar, overlooking the windswept beach as the sun set, talking intently over gin and tonics and pre-Castro Cuban cigars. Rupert, silver-haired and dressed in a blue serge suit, was as elegant as any of Russell's world-famous clients, and he knew everyone in power from both the old and the new governments. He had colorful anecdotes and descriptions for all of them, including Jomo and Ngina Kenyatta, the new president and his power-hungry, kleptomaniac wife.

"Your poacher is quite correct. They're all protected now, nothing gets sold here without somebody's consent. We're just beginning to see what I think will be the future for our wildlife. It won't be pretty. Some species—rhinos, for instance—could be completely wiped out. The Asians will pay a fortune for one bloody horn."

Russell sat there, refusing to let the idea of it sink in totally. He wanted to make sure he'd exhausted all possible alternatives.

"But what about the laws on the books? Will no one prosecute them anymore?"

Matthews answered with a soft laugh. "Russell, my friend, it's the *government* that's protecting them. They're the ones taking the biggest cut. Hell, Mama Kenyatta's even said to be involved. I believe it." He leaned back and let out a mouthful of smoke. "There's a group of us who aren't too happy about this. We'd love to have you on board if you'd like to help."

Russell let the words slip before he even thought of the possible consequences.

"Count me in. Whatever I can do. I can probably round up a few of my friends in the trade, if that would help."

Rupert smiled slyly. "Oh, we're already reaching out to some of your mates. I was about to contact you when you called." He paused momentarily. "But like your poacher said, it might cost you all your jobs. Fighting a crooked government can be very unhealthy to one's income if one loses."

"If one loses," Russell answered quietly, looking out at the hotel's flags snapping in the wind. "If one does nothing it'll cost us our jobs anyway. We'll lose our best big game, and there'll be a hit on the tourist trade like we haven't seen since the Uprising."

He finished the rest of his drink, set it down, and looked Rupert in the eyes.

"This is all I have, Rupert. It's who I am. I'm damn well not going to go down without a fight."

* * *

The first skirmish in this new war came even sooner than Russell anticipated. Ten days later, as he and Jean were overseeing final preparations for a two-week hunting safari that was to begin the next day, a call came over the radio from Ian Masterson. A bush pilot flying clients from Amboseli to Nairobi had spotted suspicious activity as he passed over the southern border of Tsavo. Several figures had run when they heard the plane approaching and ducked under some acacia trees.

The pilot had pretended not to see them or their rifles—meaning he hadn't circled back for an exploratory pass—and then, seconds later, he flew over what the men were presumably after: a herd of roughly twenty elephants making their way across a savanna, unaware that there was mortal danger right behind them.

After reassuring Jean that there would be no foolish heroics, Russell called to Kagwe and Mathu, loaded rifles and boxes of ammunition into the Land Rover, and they all raced out along the road to the south of the poachers. This kind of engagement—doing the dirty work on the ground—was the piece of the puzzle Russell and several other hunter-guides had signed on for with Rupert and his high-placed friends, who would approach the matter from a more refined, back-room political angle. But they would work in concert.

Masterson and his trackers had agreed to come in from the riverbed to the north, where it was presumed the elephants were heading, but they were a good thirty minutes further away. Russell would deal with the poachers in the most minimal way possible until Masterson arrived, starting with warning shots fired over their heads. It was up to the interlopers to set the rules of engagement from there.

Russell left the main road and headed north across an ascending plateau that would get them near the location as quickly as possible. Russell wanted to prevent any carnage, if it wasn't already too late, but he knew the odds of that were slim.

Several minutes later they came to the top of the plateau and now could see vast herds below; zebra, wildebeest, giraffe and gazelle dotted a savanna that stretched to a distant set of hills. Mathu was standing in back in the traditional place for the game spotter—his torso above the roof's hatch, giving him a 360 degree view.

Suddenly he ducked down into the cabin and whistled. Russell braked and followed Mathu's arm. On the horizon, the silhouettes of a herd of elephants were now visible about two miles away, running hard.

Russell raised his binoculars, swung them back in the direction the elephants were running from. Several hundred yards behind them he saw the dark, unmistakable shapes of men. Four of them were pursuing the herd, bounding through the tall grass. Several hundred yards further back he saw another poacher, but he was not running. His arm was moving up and down in the unmistakable arc of a swinging machete. A large grey shape like a boulder rose above the grass. Russell cursed aloud.

"Mathu! Put one over their heads. Use the .375."

Kagwe handed the big game rifle up to Mathu, who quickly shouldered the gun, flipped the safety off, and found the lead poacher in his sights. He aimed ten feet above his head and squeezed the trigger.

The report rocked the cab, but Russell knew that was nothing compared to what the bullet did when it passed over the poachers' heads. The shockwave of a large bore shell makes a loud, sizzling crack that is highly recognizable to anyone who has ever been down range of a big gun.

All four men stopped in their tracks and instinctively crouched, then heard the rifle's report a second later. Their heads whirled now, their eyes scanning the landscape for the shooter. But the Land Rover was tan-colored, and Russell had turned the wheel so the sun wouldn't reflect off the windshield.

Russell called up to Mathu as he put the vehicle back in drive.

"Stay down until we get close." He then started across the terrain toward the elephants, intending to get between the herd and the poachers.

All three men in the Land Rover knew that this was a dangerous move, but they were prepared for it. Kagwe chambered a 300 Win Mag with mounted scope and passed it up to Russell in the front seat, then loaded his own. A half mile away, the poachers spotted the Rover. When one of them raised his rifle, Kagwe shouted.

"Boss, they shoot!"

Russell stepped on the gas and they all crouched low in their seats. Then came the loud clang of a bullet slamming into the front passenger door panel. Russell kept going, at an angle that gave the poachers the smallest target, and headed for a raised outcropping of boulders.

Another bullet, this time through a rear window, and glass exploded through the cab. Russell raised his head just enough to see over the dash and realized they had reached the rocks. He braked, and all three men jumped out as a cloud of dust settled over them. They took up positions in the rocks.

"Fire until they surrender," said Russell as he slipped the safety off his Win Mag.

They had an advantage in height and they had cover. It was no match, even as the poachers fired off rounds from their position hidden in the tall grass. Russell homed in on the lead poacher, whose shape he could decipher through the scope 400 yards away. He aimed one foot above his head, knowing the bullet would lose trajectory at this distance, and squeezed off a round.

Russell saw an explosion of dust fly off the man's shirt and then he disappeared. He saw the man behind him call in panic to his downed comrade. With a .300 magnum shell, any wound was likely going to be fatal.

Now Mathu's .375 boomed from the rocks above Russell and the second man tumbled backwards. Russell could see him clutching his right leg as he rolled over, and Russell called to his trackers.

"Hold your fire. They're finished."

No sooner had he said this then the other two poachers stood up with their hands held high, their rifles thrown to the ground.

A rasp of static burst from the radio console. It was Ian. "Russell, we've found a vehicle hidden off the main road, what is your position? Over."

Russell clambered down and reached into the cab, picked up the handset.

"Two of them are down, two more have surrendered. There's at least one more, possibly armed and on his way to the vehicle, so be careful. We'll radio you on our way out, over."

From the spotter's perch, Mathu kept his .375 leveled at the two men as the Rover approached them. Fifty yards away, Kagwe jumped out and signaled them to walk forward and then drop to their knees. They looked young and scared, not the hardened men Russell had expected.

"Who's the Boss here?" demanded Russell in Kikuyu as he stepped out. Both men pointed at their downed comrades, and it was apparent they were telling the truth. Russell walked over to the two wounded men and saw the one he had shot lying in a puddle of blood, his eyes unseeing, his last breaths expelling the frothy bright blood of a lung wound. He was older than the others, maybe thirty-five. Russell suddenly felt a pang of regret, his adrenaline and hot anger replaced by remorse. But he also knew these men would have gladly killed him if the fight had gone the other way.

The second man was writhing silently, his leg a shattered mess, blood pulsing through his fingers as he held the wound. He appeared to be in his late twenties, a good ten years older than the other two. Russell aimed his rifle at the man's healthy leg.

"All right, I'm only going to ask you once, then I'm going to ruin your other knee. You'll never walk again." The man nearly cried on the spot. Russell kept his voice cold. "Who hired you? Who was going to pay you for this ivory? Was it our friend Gichinga Kimathi?"

The man looked confused at this name. Russell slammed the bolt home and the man closed his eyes. Russell fired into the dirt below his leg and the poacher shouted.

"I don't know anyone by that name! We are just hunters!"

Russell swung his rifle at the other two and they crouched in fear. One of them blurted, "We don't know anything, we are just poor farmers with families to feed!"

Russell could hear the truth in their voices; they were clearly scared out of their wits and would have given up a name if they had one. He lifted his rifle. He was shaking inside, but he couldn't let them see it.

"All right. But I have a message for you and all your friends: We're going to be watching for you. If any of you step foot in any of the preserves around here, my friends and I will hunt you down. And next time we'll show you no mercy. Is that understood?"

The men didn't make eye contact as they nodded quickly. With that Russell signaled to Kagwe and Mathu, who collected the men's rifles, and then the three of them got back in the vehicle. As they sped off, they saw the two younger poachers run to their stricken comrades.

That made Russell feel even worse; he had shot men before, it was true, but he had never seen the results lying in front of him. This was not something he'd bargained for, and now he wasn't so sure he could go through with it.

When they got to the downed elephant they saw that it had been a mature female, which meant she probably had several offspring in the herd who would miss her dearly. Her tusks had been left where the fifth poacher had dropped them when he fled. The brutality of the act, the pained, surprised look in the mother's eyes as she lay there, made even a hardened hunter like Russell want to cry. His emotions were so confusing that he felt light-headed and had to brace himself against the vehicle.

They collected the tusks and sped off in the direction the man had run. His tracks disappeared in a rocky streambed with brush covering the banks. He could be hiding in there anywhere, thought Russell, and he was probably armed.

Russell decided it wasn't worth going in after him; he didn't want to endanger his or his trusted trackers' lives, and he certainly didn't want any more violence. Anyway, the message had been delivered. So he swung the Rover around, picked up the two-way handset and headed for the main road.

"Ian, we're coming out. Give us your location, over."

* * *

Amanda set the needle down on the worn vinyl album and lay back on her bed as a nearly full moon lit her room. She had seen them on the BBC broadcast six months ago while at her school in Nairobi; had seen the hysteria, the shrieking and tears of the audience, and felt she was looking at the rest of the world through the wrong end of a telescope. Terence had sent her the album from London, and she had played it so incessantly that it had become part of her DNA.

The previous fall, she and her schoolmates had been shocked by the assassination of the young, handsome American president. A few days later, when her father returned from a safari with a wealthy Texas oilman and some of his friends, he told Jean and Amanda a disturbing story over dinner. When the news had reached them of the assassination, the clients had celebrated with cigars and champagne, and Russell had watched in dismay, silently appalled. There was a divide in the world which he had never experienced before, he confided to his wife and daughter, and it scared him. How could otherwise seemingly intelligent, sane people toast to their own president's death, he asked? What was happening in the world? Had it always been like this, but he had just chosen not to see it?

Amanda may not have understood everything her parents spoke of that evening, but she was more precocious than most girls her age, so she picked up enough to trouble her sleep that night. Every new generation has a way of rejecting the older one with their own style and music, she knew this instinctively, but this time—she could feel it in the air—the world was going to experience a sea change like nothing that had come before. She didn't know what it was going to look like, but she knew it was coming, and she wanted to be a part of it.

Terence may have been closer to the epicenter of this change, but fifty miles north of London in a bone-cold winter, trapped in a monastic boarding school teeming with testosterone and small cruelties, he might as well have been living on the moon. Adolescence is cruel, even in the best of circumstances, but without parents, or even girls to mitigate it, the toll was unfathomable. Terence had never experienced the kind of bullying that went on at a school like Bedford. The upper classmen could get to you anywhere, and since the lower classmen never dared speak up, they did so with impunity. Like humiliating you publicly with lacerating comments about your masculinity that sent those within earshot into convulsions of sniggering. Or sprinkling dead flies on your dinner in the dining hall. Or tossing your dorm room and drenching your pillow with urine. Why were they picking on him, Terence wondered impotently? What did they see in him to deserve this kind of ridicule? He had always been popular at his old school, was athletic and not bad-looking in the bargain. But none of those qualities meant anything with these ruthless, cunning boys who were the inheritors of their families' great wealth, power and status. Terence had tried not to show any weakness, like his father had counseled, but these bullies could scent anybody's fears or frailties, and they pursued their victims like bloodhounds. He couldn't shake them. Nobody could shake them.

Terence would lay in bed at night listening to the wind roar outside the ancient brick dormitory, his thoughts filled with dark scenarios of revenge, of rejoinders he could never summon in the light of day. Eventually he would dissolve into tears and then give himself a small release before falling into a sleep that never seemed to renew him.

His situation was not something he dared communicate to his parents five-thousand miles away lest he alarm his mother—or disappoint his father. He answered his mother's weekly letters with cheery versions of his days and his friendships, and of his studies, which were suffering from a temporary dyslexia brought on by the trauma of his circumstances. There were no counselors in those days, and boys didn't even know to reach out for help, so a good many of them sank beneath the waves, only to resurface years later with scars that they would pass on to their own sons and daughters.

The British system of boys' boarding schools would not begin to change until the 1970s, when girls were finally admitted and teachers were taught to recognize, and counsel, struggling students. The system that had damaged so many lives would not be missed.

CHAPTER SEVEN

Zambia—Present Day

THE ROTORS OF THE Eurocopter SA 315 were approaching full speed as Trevor Blackmon climbed into the passenger seat with his .416 Rigby and a laptop. He slipped on the headset so he could converse with the pilot, a trusted friend from their days together in the Rhodesian Bush War, and belted himself in. It was already late afternoon, and they would have to cover the thirty miles to their target and locate him in the forest he was apparently following before night fell, or they would have to return in the morning. That could prove problematic. The elephant might be on the outskirts of Kabwe by the next day, and then all bets would be off.

The call from the satellite tracking office had come as a welcome surprise: Yes, in fact there had been a chip implanted in a mature bull who was now unaccounted for. He hadn't come from Lower Zambezi Park, as Blackmon had first surmised, but from a private game preserve run by naturalists for the wealthy scion of an American distillery.

The electrified fence surrounding the twenty thousand-acre preserve had been breached and the elephant had disappeared; the breach had only been discovered three days ago when several younger bulls had wandered out and caused a panic in the nearby settlement. But the naturalists thought the old bull had been gone for perhaps a week, and they would greatly appreciate it if the authorities could "round him up" and hold him until a team could be sent to transport him back.

How, Blackmon thought, was he supposed to round up and hold a fifteen thousand-pound bull that had gone rogue? Dart him? If the tranquilizer didn't work right away, he would thunder off in a dangerous rage. And if everything *did* go according to plan, what, they'd just chain him to a tree before he woke up? The most powerful animal in the world? He'd smash almost any tree to the ground and walk away dragging what was left of it, and that would probably *really* piss him off. Blackmon could see the outcome of most of these scenarios, including the possible loss of life and the certain loss of his job—and he wasn't going to go near them. No, he thought as they lifted off and the airfield disappeared below them, there was only one sure-fire solution, and this was it.

* * *

I awoke from a shallow sleep as the forest around me came alive with the first stirrings of the night creatures: all the little friends who hoot and howl, and the invisible ones who are the pulsing heart of the night.

I'd been traveling in the forest since the day before—when I had sensed the two-leggers' presence all around me—so by now my stomach ached with hunger. I began searching for something soft to fill my gut, but since no grasses grow in the shade of a forest, I had to go looking at the edge of it, hoping to find a meadow.

As I approached the place where the trees thinned—it was sundown by now—I got a strange, overwhelming feeling of dread. I don't know where these visions come from, and it is only in my old age that they have begun to visit me—but they have never led me astray. So, even though the night creatures were still singing loudly, I heeded it and backed deeper into the forest again.

At that very moment I heard the low throbbing of a two-leggers' false bird. It was flying low, just above the treetops, which I now know is how they approach when they mean to rain down death. If they fly high above, they only mean to pass quickly by, and have no business with us down here.

I have seen these false birds kill entire herds with their boom sticks, and it is a horror to behold. Families racing in and out of the trees, desperately trying to get away, but the huge birds just hover above them, killing one after the other until they've all been silenced.

So I stood under the tallest, densest trees I could find and stayed very still. The tree creatures screeched as the branches above them whipped around from the wind of the false bird. It was coming closer and closer, as if somehow it knew I was in this very place, and then it stopped above me. I knew I had to stay still—to run would mean my death.

Blackmon peered down at the canopy in the dusk, his eyes trying to pick out the elephant's shape a hundred feet below. He could see the GPS' icon blinking on the laptop, it had to be somewhere right below them, but he was having the damndest time seeing it through the treetops. This was a full, mature forest with trees topping out at sixty feet, and he had the sneaking suspicion this bull knew it.

"Take it down to treetop level, maybe we can get him to run," he shouted into his mic. The pilot took them down until the skids almost sat on the treetops. Blackmon shouldered the Rigby and peered down through the scope, sweeping the rifle slowly from side to side. Nothing was moving except frightened birds and monkeys; the old bull hadn't broken into a run.

Out of frustration, and perhaps due to the anabolic steroids he had been taking to increase his workout loads, Blackmon fired a round. Maybe that would get him to move.

"You see him?" asked the pilot. Blackmon didn't answer; he was concentrating on the forest floor, but still there was no elephant.

"Try the flood!" Blackmon barked. The pilot flipped a switch and the nose-mounted floodlight popped on. He toggled it around, aiming it through the swirling branches. But that made the visual even worse, creating a blinding glow off the leaves and a crazy, swooning pattern on the forest floor. And still, nothing moved but the panicked monkeys.

* * *

Even though adrenaline coursed through his veins, the old bull stood as still as a statue. The sound and fury was so close, so loud, he didn't even realize the rifle had been fired until a hot pain shot down through his left shoulder. He didn't know what it was at first, but as it became more and more painful, he realized with a sick wave of shock—literally—that this had come from a boomstick.

He sank to his knees slowly, leaning against the trunk of the massive tree, and closed his eyes. He felt for the wound with the tip of his trunk. He smelled blood, then felt the slippery, oozing wound where the enemy had entered him. He knew what could happen, he had seen it too many times not to know. He had to remain calm. If he waited, he could survive this.

And then the sound and fury suddenly abated. The false bird's searching light turned away, blinked off, and then the false bird itself roared away. In seconds its sound was gone, and the chattering and pulsing of the forest gradually returned. The elephant rose to its feet unsteadily and looked around in the gloaming. Well, this was going to make the journey more complicated, he thought, but he had survived worse. He was going to have to find a mud hole and fill the wound, that was the first thing on his mind. Now, everything would have to be about surviving. Food would have to wait.

CHAPTER EIGHT

Kenya and London, 1965

FOUR MONTHS AFTER the first wild herd passed by Salisbury Farm and informed Ishi of the fate of his birth family, he was in the middle of a deep sleep when a rumbling sound reached him and made his eyes pop open. As his head cleared he realized the rumbling was not in his dream, it was real—another wild herd was passing in the night. He looked over at his young zebra friend, who continued to sleep, and realized that no other animals could hear the sound. He stealthily got to his feet and slipped outside.

He had studied how the humans opened and closed the sliding bolt on the outside of the stockade's gate for some time now, so it was just a matter of seconds before he slid it open with his trunk, which is very possibly the most dexterous "limb" in the animal kingdom.

Even though this wild herd was a complete unknown—he couldn't hear enough of their voices to tell whether they were friendly or not—he knew he had to take the chance or it might not come again. A gnawing desire had taken hold inside him in the last months, a powerful longing to wander the plains and rivers with his own kind. As much as he still loved the two-leggers who had raised him, he didn't want to be isolated behind a fence with animals who were so different from him, who could not speak to him except through crude gestures.

He nudged the heavy sliding gate open and slipped through the opening, then trotted quickly down the hill. A few minutes later he caught sight of them in the darkness up ahead. Their pace was typical of a night journey, all of them bunched closely and foregoing browsing until the next rest and feed stop.

Ishi fell in at the rear and had gone about a mile with them when the female watching over the last of the herd's young suddenly swung around and stopped in her tracks. There was no moon up, so she stared with apparent confusion—and then realized this little male did not have a scent she recognized. Before she could raise the alarm, Ishi spoke up quietly.

"Sorry, I didn't mean to startle you."

The female stared, her ears fanned out warily, then gave a low rumbling call to the matriarch at the front of the herd.

"Mother Blue, we have a stranger tagging along with us. Better come see."

All the elephants turned now, and the matriarch walked back along the line as they gathered around the new arrival. Ishi felt every last eye on him and, despite the many hours he'd rehearsed in his head about how he would win over his new "family"—whenever they appeared—he piddled uncontrollably.

He expected derision and laughter, so the reaction he got was a surprise. Most of the herd's hearts went out to him, and several of the young calves urinated in sympathy. Mother Blue stared down at Ishi; there was kindness in her eyes, but also a wariness.

"What is your name, little one? And where have you come from?"

"My name is—well, my name won't mean anything to you, it was given to me by the two-leggers. They're the ones back at the nest you just passed. They call me Ishi."

"Mmm. And what does this—" she had a difficult time forming the word—"'Ishi' name mean?"

"I—I don't really know," he stammered. "I don't speak their language. But they are very kind. They've cared for me as if they were my own family."

"And where is your family?"

Ishi lowered his eyes. "They…are just bones now. They were killed by two-leggers three rainy seasons ago. And then these kind two-leggers took me in." Several trunks reached out to touch him, and he was wrapped in a warmth and caring he'd forgotten since his first days with his birth family.

Another voice rumbled from beside Mother Blue—an old cow who was stooped and grizzled and had a personality to match.

"So now you've decided to leave them, eh? If they've been so kind, if you have no family left, maybe you should show them some gratitude and stay there!"

"Thorn Tree, leave the little one alone," chided Mother Blue, who then addressed Ishi again, but she was speaking to all the herd. "It is every one of our kind's right to roam free. In fact it is an abomination to be kept from the natural life. We honor your choice to leave the two-leggers. And unless there are any objections, you are welcomed to our clan for as long you choose to stay."

She stood back and raised her trunk in the air, waiting for the go-ahead. The clan all looked from this lost little three-year old to their matriarch—and, except for Thorn Tree, who abstained, all raised their trunks and rumbled their approval.

"Very well, little one. As long as you can feed yourself and keep up with us, you may come along." Mother Blue turned and headed back to the front of the line as two very friendly male calves placed Ishi between them in the line.

"But, my goodness," Mother Blue rumbled, "we're going to have to do something about that name."

* * *

Kamau was the first to realize something was amiss. Since he no longer needed to sleep with Ishi—the calf had been on his own at night for months now—he had come from his room off the garage to get his morning tea by the cook's fire when he realized the gate was wide open. There were no escapees lurking outside, so he slid it closed and secured the bolt, then raised the alarm.

All the keepers came running, and then Jean had them take a head count. Of all the orphans, only Ishi and a baby warthog were missing. It didn't take long to round up the warthog, who was cowering in the nearby forest beneath a family of loud, menacing baboons, but Ishi was another matter. They found where his tracks met up with the herd's and realized with dawning certainty that he had jimmied the gate and taken off with them.

Even though this was the day one always hoped for—that your charge had grown mature enough to join a natural family in the wild—it always came with an avalanche of worry. Could they survive on their own? Would they be easy prey without their caregivers watching over them? This was Jean's first elephant calf to make it this far, so it hit her especially hard.

"Kamau, find Kagwe and have him bring the .375," she said as she headed for the Land Rover. "I want to make sure he's OK." Russell was away on safari and would never have allowed Jean to leave without protection, so Kagwe was the best alternative.

It's not exactly complicated to track a herd of elephants, thought Jean as she drove the three of them; it's where the old saying comes from. Where there are no trees, they leave a path of pungent scat and flattened earth; where there are trees, they usually leave a swath of broken limbs, trunks stripped of bark, sometimes whole trees uprooted and laying on the ground. So it was just after ten in the morning—three hours after Kamau had first made the discovery—that they caught up with the herd. They were in a mud wallow left over from a stream that was about to disappear until the next rainy season.

* * *

Mother Blue heard the engine first and lifted her ears and trunk to locate it in the tinder-dry brush and twisted myrrh trees nearby. Soon all the other females were aware of it, and they circled the calves in a protective formation as they searched the air for its fuel scent. The egrets who had been atop their backs, picking insects and nuggets of vegetation from their mud-covered hides, took flight.

Then the tires crunched loudly over some stones about 200 meters away and they all turned to face it. The false beast was coming slowly, so it was seeking them. Then it stopped.

The two-legger poking through the beast's top was staring right at them, but he gave off no scent of danger. Then the beasts's two sides opened and a pair of two-leggers stepped out. Mother Blue gauged the distance and thought she could cover the ground in a matter of twenty strides if necessary.

She sensed movement behind her and the new calf bolted out from the protective circle, trunk raised, and stared at the creatures. Then, if an elephant can smile, Ishi did.

"They are my two-leggers!" he shouted to his new herd. "You have nothing to fear from them." And with that he ran towards the false beast, followed by the two calves who'd befriended him the night before. Their mothers trumpeted angrily and stormed out to cut them off, leaving Ishi on his own.

Jean walked out and opened her arms, whereupon Ishi rubbed his face up against her tenderly, his trunk caressing her legs, back, and then her head. Jean was surprised to find herself laughing while simultaneously crying, even as her clothes were now wet and filthy, and she buried her face in his.

Kamau was next, and Ishi nudged him so forcefully Kamau almost fell over before finding his footing and pushing back. Kamau laughed with delight.

"My goodness, you have become such a big boy now, eh? You are ready to go off on your own, and leave us all with holes in our hearts?"

Ishi turned and looked back at his herd, realizing for the first time that they hadn't moved, they were just watching in the distance.

"Does no one want to meet my two-legger friends?" he asked. "They are quite friendly…"

The older females demurred. The general rule was that a healthy relationship with a two-legger meant a healthy amount of distance between them.

"No," rumbled Mother Blue, "you say your goodbyes, little one, we'll be waiting for you on the trail."

Jean would probably have gone out in the Land Rover for several more days to keep an eye on his progress, but an urgent message from London prevented such overly-maternal behavior, and she watched forlornly as Ishi trotted off to rejoin his new herd. Then the elephants fell into their pre-assigned formation, filed up the riverbank, and disappeared in the trees.

* * *

Jean tried to sleep in the darkened cabin of the BOAC Boeing 707 as it made its way across the North African night, but the information she'd heard fading in and out over the shortwave was so alarming that sleep was out of the question.

What little she understood was that Terence had been running down his dormitory's stairwell when he fell headlong into a cast iron radiator on one of the landings. Most of his front teeth had been broken, his jaw dislocated and lips and mouth badly lacerated, and the school had rushed him to a London specialist to undergo oral and plastic surgery.

Jean could only imagine the pain and anguish her son must be in, so she telephoned her parents at their country home in Staffordshire, who hastily jumped in their car and started the seventy-mile drive to London as Jean boarded her flight from Nairobi. Russell was on safari and, even if he'd been available, wouldn't have flown to be by his son's side. In those days, that was seen as a mother's duty.

Jean had always questioned sending her son a continent away, but never raised her concerns with her husband because that was how things were done. If you came from a good family, it was expected that you would go away to a British boarding school if you were a boy, or to a Swiss boarding school if you were a girl. To not go away would raise awkward questions.

So now, after five months at Bedford and two plaintive letters—addressed to her, not to Russell—Jean was distraught. He had confided to her that he was being teased mercilessly for being "fay," and the winter was so unendingly cold and rainy that he was deeply depressed. And now this.

Looking back on this period from several years on, Jean was able to see the first cracks in her marriage but, like all happy unions that go off the rails in their second or third decade, she didn't recognize them at the time. The small resentments that she put in a drawer and shut away grew over the years until they burst from their darkness. The way upper class mothers had to quietly go along with their husbands' decisions—for instance having little say in how their kids were schooled—was just the first crack.

And the biggest of all was starting to grow now, but they both ignored the signs. Jean was too passive in her questioning of why Russell had to make his living, and his reputation, as a professional hunter when several of his compatriots were now making just as much money leading photographic-only safaris. The irony was stunning: here Jean was, raising orphaned animals whose mothers had been killed by hunters, yet her husband was one of the most sought-after hunters in Africa.

The resentment began as a pain in her chest that silently grew and spread each time she broached the subject, and his responses grew more defensive and strident.

"You knew who I was when you married me, what gives you the right to make me feel guilty about who I am *now?* About how I make my living?"

The silences after these talks were long and heavy, not only because this was tied to his identity as a male, but because it was the essential difference between the two of their philosophies, even their personalities.

How, she thought now as the airliner began its descent over the Channel, would they even be able to stay together—as friends, as parents, as lovers—when their differences were so profound?

* * *

Terence's jaw was wired shut and the whites of his eyes were filled with blood in a face grotesquely swollen and bruised, so it was everything Jean could do to remain composed when she saw him.

The school official who had accompanied him to London was in the dark about what exactly had transpired to cause the accident, and Jean's parents hadn't broached the subject. But when Jean sat alone with her son that night, he wrote a note in his sedated haze and handed it to her.

Once she realized what the words were saying, she was shocked and then angered. He was her son, and she had allowed him to be thrown to the wolves.

"I was pushed," it said, "by some mean older boys. They'll deny it, but it's the truth."

She tried to stay calm as she quizzed him, and after a few minutes the facts came out. There had been a crush of students hurriedly descending the stairs to get to the dining hall for breakfast when he was tripped from behind, and his hands barely broke his fall. The lead perpetrator was sixteen, an oversized bully who ruled a small clique of rich, well-connected scions.

When she later inquired about the boy from the school official—Jean made sure to sound oblivious—it turned out he came from the family of a powerful minister of parliament whose name was well-known to anyone who read the papers. He was a right-wing Tory who regularly made the news with ugly rhetoric directed primarily at the first wave of Pakistani immigrants coming into Britain, so it made perfect sense to Jean that his son would be a bully as well.

When she asked Terence if he wanted to confront the clique and have them punished, or just get on a plane and come home, he wrote one word on his notepad and clutched her hands beseechingly.

"Home."

As she slept fitfully in the chair beside his bed that night, she realized she would be battling the school as well as her husband, who would want his son to stay at Bedford and not be a "quitter." And the school would refute the accusation unless there was a witness, and she knew there would be none: Terence was considered a weakling whom no teenaged male would stick his neck out for. He was on his own.

That realization was what clinched it for her. No matter what anyone tried to persuade her of, she had to get him out. And get some of their money back, because throwing away the tuition was more than they could afford to lose, especially with Amanda starting school in Switzerland the next year.

Jean smiled at that thought as she finally fell asleep: At least she didn't have to worry about her daughter. Amanda was so fierce and headstrong, no one would dare bully her.

* * *

It was an uneasy truce in the beginning, but Russell finally came around to the wisdom of his wife's decision, and after the visible damage to their son's face and mouth had subsided, Terence returned to the safety and familiarity of his Nairobi school with his father's approval, if not his delight.

The matter of his masculinity, or at least the accusations coming from a clique of cruel adolescent boys, was not spoken of again.

Then, as if in answer to a prayer she had never dared to ask, as if there had been a glitch in the heavens, one of the other "sons" she held so dear returned home unexpectedly. And, just like Terence, he too had been wounded by predators.

CHAPTER NINE

Kenya, Switzerland, 1965

EVEN AS I BEGAN TO *know the personalities and quirks of my new clan, as the long, hot days of the dry season stretched on, I felt a gnawing ache in my heart, but I didn't recognize the reason at first. It only crept up on me at night, when the travails of the day subsided and one had the time to ruminate, so I was able to keep it at bay.*

The morning began without any indication that things might be different. The heat was intense even before dawn, and as the orb rose we could see that there had been more deaths among the plains-dwellers. They were mostly the very young and the very old, but their families could hardly show their grief, there was so much work to be done just to stay alive. Which was why they stayed close to us, or any elephants they could, because our adults could scent water even when a streambed was parched and buried under sand.

Our females would dig and kick a hole until the dark, cool earth underneath gave up its moisture, and the adults would fill their trunks from the seepage and then empty them in our mouths. After the herd had had its fill, the plains-dwellers would descend on the trampled, muddy holes and lick the last moisture until it was just sand again.

Even the predators were desperate, a lesson I had not yet learned. They could not replenish their fluids by drinking the blood of their kills alone; they too needed water. I had been taught the rules of survival by my mother, but the repetition that would become habitual had not taken effect when I lost her, and the two-leggers could not be expected to teach me.

As I wandered away with my two new mates after our morning water, waiting for the herd to form up for the day's travels, we weren't paying close attention to our sightlines as we wrestled and bumped each other.

We settled in the shade of some fever trees and hardly noticed as a family of warthogs bolted from the dried grass nearby. Then the musky scent of a big cat washed over me and I looked up at my mates. Their eyes were wide with alarm too, and we looked about to see where our protectors were. We had been so oblivious when we wandered off that we couldn't see them, nor they us.

In that instant the predator sprang from her hiding place. I felt her hit me so hard that I staggered, then felt her claws digging into my side and head, then smelled her breath as she sank her teeth into my neck. I couldn't cry out, but I later learned that my friends had raised the alarm.

I had seen enough death by that age to recognize the shock that clouds a victim's decisions, like the way their eyes glass over and they accept the coming of the end. I had always promised myself I would not succumb to it, that I would fight if my time came. I rolled over desperately, trying to dislodge her. She grunted loudly as all my weight crashed down on her, then she let go and quickly grabbed me again, this time on my exposed belly. I kicked at her stomach and heard her exhale painfully, but it didn't dislodge her.

All of a sudden she was lifted into the air and I saw Mother Blue's trunk wrapped around her tail. The cat screamed and lunged at Mother Blue, but Mother Blue swung her around so she couldn't reach her, then slammed her violently to the ground. Then slammed her down again, then one last time, then heaved her far into the air.

When the lioness landed she didn't jump to her feet like injured cats usually do, she just twitched violently and laid still, her bones shattered, her neck crushed. I let out the most pitiable cry I think an elephant ever did, then rolled over and staggered to my feet.

"Little One, are you hurt?" Mother Blue implored, running her trunk over my body, sniffing to see how deep the wounds were. I now realized almost all the females were there as well, snorting and trumpeting fiercely at the rest of the lioness' family, which had come running. Facing a row of powerful, angry elephants, they quickly withdrew and waited a safe distance away.

Now the pain of the wounds hit me, and I realized that little drops of red were raining down from my head and I think I passed out, because when I awoke, I was lying in the shade of a rock outcropping and several females were tending to my wounds. They were packing mud mixed with flame tree flowers in my wounds, but the salve hardly made the pain any better.

I saw my two playmates staring at me in worry, and realized something really bad had caught their eye.

"What is it?" I asked weakly.

"Your...your ear," said the one known as Sad Eyes. I wagged my ears and felt a sharp pain in my left one, and then I saw that it had been torn partly off and was just hanging there, limp. I gasped with anguish and surprise, and as hard as all the females were trying, I understood with a bolt of certainty what the ache in my heart had been about, and what I now had to do.

* * *

The sight of the elephants coming up the hill in the heat seemed like a mirage to Kamau as he collected kindling in the trees just outside the compound, but it was definitely elephants, and they were headed right for Salisbury. Kamau darted inside the gate and whistled to his fellow keepers, then rapped on the main residential quarters.

"Mama Jean! Come quickly!"

As he stepped back outside, he was startled to see a very familiar form breaking away from the adults—there were six of them in all—and run towards him. The young elephant's left ear was hanging uselessly and he was covered in dried blood, but it was clearly Ishi.

"Oh, Ishi, what has happened to you?" Kamau called, and then Jean was beside him as well, and she gasped at the sight. Ishi stopped just short of them and lowered his head in a gesture of submissiveness and helplessness.

Jean called into the compound's yard. "Mathu, get Hillary on the radio and tell him we need him immediately!" The claw marks were long and livid, the bite wounds were deep, blood-filled punctures that would require cleansing and stitches, as would the ear, or the infection would be disastrous. The humans gathered him in and escorted him into the compound.

Kamau was about to close the gate when he turned and saw that two of the adult elephants had moved closer and were standing not twenty paces away. He stopped and looked them in the eye, then slowly opened his arms in a gesture of friendship.

"If you stay right there, we will be happy to get you some feed and water…"

He nodded to the remaining keepers, who were watching from inside the gate, and the men scurried off to the feed shed. The two elephants barely took their eyes off Kamau, and he too did not move. When the keepers reappeared, they would not venture out past the gate.

"As long as we move slowly," Kamau whispered to them, "they won't hurt us." One of them had his arms full of sweet long grass; the other two were lugging a barrel of water. They set them down beside Kamau and retreated.

Kamau gathered up two handfuls of the grass and took a couple of cautious steps towards the giant beasts, whose trunks were now swinging from side to side and sniffing at the air. Kamau raised a handful of grass, and then his heart did a flip—the biggest of the two started moving towards him, her smell and size overwhelming, and suddenly Kamau had grave doubts about his bravura gesture. His breath caught in his throat as the elephant reached her trunk out. Kamau opened his hand and let her take the grass, which she did with the utmost gentleness. Then she stuffed it in her mouth and started chewing, her eyes never leaving his.

He was all in now, so he raised the other hand and offered it as well. The female rumbled something in her throat and stood back; the movement startled Kamau, but he couldn't show it for fear of spooking her.

Now the second female sidled around the first and took the handful of grass. The keepers behind the gate were frozen in awe and delight, none of them realizing how loud Kamau's heart was thumping in his chest.

These two females seemed to be the most trusting of the group—the others would not approach—so Kamau had the keepers leave the food and water just outside the gate and then they all retreated inside.

Within moments, all of the elephants were eating and drinking the offerings, and it was gone in seconds. The keepers rushed back to the shed for more, and this time one of them ventured out with Kamau to feed their guests.

Kamau would never forget this day, even years later after he'd traveled with Ishi and his herd in the wild for weeks at a time. This was the day that he learned he truly had a gift for being among them, these powerful, complex creatures, a gift he would employ for the rest of his life.

Ishi's herd mates left the next morning, after Ishi's sedation had worn off and they were able to have a conversation with him over the fence. Mother Blue was the only one of them who had seen bandages before, so she explained that this was customary with two-leggers, and they all agreed that Ishi was in good hands.

They promised they would return in due time—whenever the long rains came, most likely—and they would hold him in their memories until then. Ishi was moved and grateful; these five females had left the herd and accompanied him for two long days and nights through dangerous heat to get him back to his two-leggers.

He would be able to heal and regain his strength while they made their dry season pilgrimage, and then they would come back for him. That was loyalty. That was family. That was love. Ishi knew he was a lucky elephant, now several times over.

* * *

Amanda had left for Switzerland that fall and, true to her mother's prediction, survived in spite of the cruelties visited on her fellow classmates by the older girls. Since most of the students came from great wealth—they were the daughters of the ruling class in whatever countries they came from—Amanda was considered one of the "poor" girls, since her father still worked and their family wasn't titled or famous.

Amanda was able to put off any potential tormenters by ingratiating herself to one of the most powerful, desirable girls in the school, who happened to live across the hall from her. Her father was the king of Spain, and they hit it off when Amanda came upon her in the forest one evening having an illicit smoke.

They sat watching the sun set over the mountains, with the lights of Montreux beginning to blink on far below, and after sharing several cigarettes, which Amanda for the first time inhaled, they were fast friends. Amanda's stories of Africa—of orphaned elephants, of working a farm, of her dashing father—captivated the princess, and they kept up their friend-ship until the princess' death in a climbing accident twenty years later.

Amanda wasn't particularly athletic, so her first winter on the slopes—skiing was a mandatory activity—made her a bit of a laughing-stock, as most of the girls had been flying down mountains since they were tod-dlers. She needed to find something at which she could stand out, so one day she walked into the school newspaper's office, located in a room in the basement of what had been a grand hotel in the early 20th century, and announced to the two girls sitting at their desks that she loved writing.

"And what is it that you write exactly?" asked one of them in a hon-eyed Southern United States drawl that couldn't hide a thick slice of skep-ticism.

"Anything and everything. Even poetry, if that's required."

The two girls didn't roll their eyes, which Amanda took as a good sign.

"Well, we don't require much poetry," said the second, a defiantly masculine-looking Irish girl. "What kind of training have you had?"

"Not that journalism requires much training," lobbed the southern girl.

"Well, I'm a voracious reader…and I got all A's in Creative Writing. Does that count?"

The two girls looked at each other, brows furled—and then burst into laughter.

"We were just putting you on, sweetie. What's your name?"

Amanda let her breath out in relief. "Boy, you guys had me going. I'm Amanda Hathaway, from Nairobi, Kenya."

"Well, Amanda from Nairobi," said the Irish girl as they shook hands, "I'm Jamie McGillavray from Dublin, and this is Melinda Moffet from Savannah, Georgia."

"You're hired," said Melinda as they shook.

"Ever seen a printing press?" asked Jamie, indicating one in the cor-ner. "Or a layout table?"

"Cause you're gonna spend a lot of time type-setting and printing before you get any writing assignments," added Melinda.

Amanda stared at the contraptions, trying not to show her complete ignorance.

"I'm a quick learner."

"Well, we've been waiting for you to walk in the door," smiled Jamie. "Congratulations."

It turned out that these two girls ran the paper—from writing to editing to publishing the 200 copies per week—and since they were both seniors they would be leaving it with no successors, so Amanda was a godsend. And they were a godsend to Amanda.

Since almost all the articles were puff pieces or strictly informational—school news, sports scores, profiles—and much of her time was spent type-setting and printing by hand, Amanda was bored by the end of that first winter, so she struck a deal with them.

She would be allowed to write pieces that interested her. She could only do them after she'd finished any assigned material, and only every so often. Her two bosses seemed to have no sense of what journalism could be, but not Amanda.

What made her different, and soon made her famous in the school and beyond, was her uncanny ability—even at age sixteen—to recognize a good story and then dig it out. It came from her acute sense of justice; she wouldn't quit until she was able to expose what she perceived as wrong, whether it was a trivial school matter or something in the greater world that required an editorial piece.

By her second year, when she had inherited the editorship and recruited two like-minded classmates, she went after even more controversial stories, some of which brought the angry attention of the Dean of Students. But this was the height of the '60s, and Amanda was not one to back down. Then came her coup.

One Saturday after classes, Amanda had changed out of her school uniform and was riding a local bus into Lausanne, a city of 130,000 on Lake Geneva, when a pair of young African women sat down across from her. She overheard them talking in Kiswahili, and picked up enough details to realize they were part of the underclass of workers she'd noticed from places like Turkey, Yugoslavia, Italy, and Africa; low-paid maids and kitchen staff, or day laborers, who disappeared when the sun went down. Until that moment she'd never really given it any thought, but now it hit her: there was a powerful story here if she could pull it off.

She stayed on the bus until they reached the end of the line, then got off and walked after the women as they trudged back to their lodgings.

As they turned down a dirt path between two hulking, dilapidated buildings in a seedy industrial section, the women were certain now that they were being followed, so Amanda smiled disarmingly.

"Would it be OK if I talked to you?" she asked in Kiswahili, which made both women gape in surprise. "I apologize for following you, I didn't mean to alarm you. If you'd like, I'll buy us some sweets and coffee. I just wanted to ask you about your lives here in Europe."

"What do our lives here matter to you?" asked the older of the two guardedly.

"I'm writing an essay for a class at my school," she answered, surprising herself at how easy it was to tell a half truth. "About the immigrants who've come here from all over the world to find work." She smiled innocently. "I'm from Kenya. Where are you from?"

It took a bit of evasion and subtle persuasion at first, then three more sessions as she gained the girls' trust, but Amanda eventually charmed them into a story that became an expose of the two distinct classes living together in what was supposed to be the most egalitarian country in Europe. The foreign worker community lived in terrible squalor—sometimes a dozen to a room—with their passports held by syndicates that lured them to Europe with promises of money and opportunity, only to keep them in a version of indentured servitude that was impossible to escape.

The piece was published in the school paper and, much to the administration's embarrassment, caused a storm of protest from the local business community, who wanted the piece killed, all copies of the paper destroyed, and Amanda disciplined for her lies and insolence.

But the story had already spread beyond the school and been picked up by a crusading alternative weekly in Geneva. Instead of being asked to step down from the paper—even face possible discipline—Amanda was lionized as a seventeen-year old prodigy, and the school had no choice but to stand behind her, grudgingly at first; then, when opinions poured in from across Europe, ever so proudly.

The story opened the door to a career Amanda had never known she was destined for, and, after boarding school, to a life that took her further

and further away from her African home. In the end, she would only
return to visit occasionally, but that was as it should be. She had always
wanted to become a citizen of the world, to see it through the proper end
of the telescope. And now she would.

CHAPTER TEN

Zambia and Manhattan, Present Day

THE OLD BULL HAD WALKED the entire night, hoping he might find a poultice to stem the pain and the bleeding in his shoulder, but there had been no suitable plant source, so he just filled the wound with mud. He was having trouble keeping his mind in the present, unaware that his brain was short-circuiting from the effects of the wound and its concomitant fever. In his delirium he was with his two-legged friends again as they nursed him back to health. He knew he was looking for them—it was one of the main reasons for his journey, he now remembered—but he wasn't sure how far they might be from here.

The land he was traveling through had an unfamiliar, dangerous stench to it, so he stayed as far from the two-leggers' territory as possible as he followed his internal compass north.

When the sun rose the next morning over a smoke-filled landscape choked with power lines, he realized he had made a mistake. Because now there was no more cover. No trees, no forest to hide in, only desolate fields and hills and the grey, painful-on-the-feet hardscape, and fences that sliced the land into pieces and prevented a direct route anywhere.

He could see the false beasts passing quickly in the haze below, and the noises emanating from the area were strange and alarming; an unearthly groaning, a deep thumping that shook the ground, and long, harsh calls that rent the air.

He followed a high chain link fence that led away from the foul-smelling place. His eyes stung from the clouds that billowed up from the site. Strange birds screeched overhead; black, nasty birds who now started diving at him, picking and gouging at his hide.

He had not put on a coating of mud in days, so his skin was particularly vulnerable, and his reaction time with his trunk was way too slow to keep the creatures at bay. It was an insult to such a mighty creature, but he'd survived worse, he kept telling himself; you just had to keep moving, and things around you would change soon enough.

* * *

Werner Brandeis was a man who was used to getting his way. His family's fortune, made by his grandfather in the early 20th century on the human weakness for alcohol, had given him an unfair advantage in virtually every interaction he had with people. The fact that he had a famous fortune made people behave in ways they normally never would. It also helped forgive personality traits that would usually be considered offensive. In people with his kind of money, those traits were just considered eccentric.

Brandeis had a peculiarly ageless face, made more so by having gone completely bald in his thirties, and his habit of wearing outlandish designer glasses. On good days he could pass for thirty, on stressful days he could look sixty. He was not an easy boss, husband or friend. His rages were legendary. The one weakness he had, the one soft spot in his armor, was for the defenseless. Not defenseless humans, who he pretty much blamed for whatever lot had befallen them, but defenseless animals.

"Remember," his wife reminded their friends—and it was debatable whether she was kidding—"Hitler loved his dogs."

Which was why he had bought a sixty-thousand-acre parcel of land in Zambia, surrounded it with electrified fences, and then had it stocked with every African animal his people could lay their hands on, with a concentration on threatened and endangered species.

It drove him crazy that people would hunt animals with weapons that the animals had no chance of outrunning or outwitting. If he could have had his way, the human killers would be dropped inside his fences, weaponless and without supplies, and have to figure out how to survive. That would change things quickly enough. This thought always made him smile.

So when his people came to him in the corporation's Park Avenue offices and reported that the preserve's oldest bull elephant had somehow escaped the preserve and been located hundreds of miles away, heading north through civilization, he was up out of his chair demanding answers. He had paid a small fortune some twelve years ago to have this bull shipped to the preserve, but none of these employees had been at the company then, so they knew nothing about the elephant's long and complicated history.

"Who's in charge of bringing him back? Who do we have on the scene?"

"Well, we don't actually have any of our people on site yet," said his vice president of Public Affairs, who then realized that this was probably not the answer Brandeis wanted to hear and quickly added, "They've been in contact with a warden at the national park there, and he's going to have the animal in his care as soon as possible. Hopefully by tomorrow."

"They don't have him in their care yet?" Brandeis asked incredulously. "I want this warden on the phone. And get me the Brit who's running the preserve, what's his name. Westbrook. I want our people up there *immediately*."

* * *

Trevor Blackmon was striding towards the waiting helicopter as the sun rose over the air field, its light casting long, strangely-oscillating shadows. Blackmon was so focused on his mission that he didn't see the clerk step outside the central office bungalow and wave to him, signaling that he had a phone call. Whatever the clerk shouted was lost in the roar of the rotors, something about "From America" and "Urgent," but Blackmon would have no idea this transpired until he was facing his termination hearings.

* * *

Jeremy Westbrook had what he considered to be a good relationship with the preserve's American benefactor. Whereas most people lived in fear of him, Jeremy knew his secret passion and therefore thought they had a connection, in that he was the expert on all things animal. It gave him comfort to know that Brandeis actually needed him and even deferred to him in this area.

It was in this capacity that Westbrook was being flown, along with his assistant and two of his rangers, via the preserve's helicopter to rendezvous with the national parks warden who had first been alerted to the elephant's presence in civilization. They were going to hook up with the warden outside an industrial town where the bull had last shown up on GPS and figure out how to capture him and get him transported back to the preserve.

The fact that Westbrook had insisted on implanting a chip in the elephant's hide when he first took the job made him now look prescient. Westbrook—at 39 a nice-looking man-child who women soon realized was more interested in animals than the female sex—knew they had been lucky so far: a bull this big, with tusks as heavy as his, would be priceless to any poacher. That much ivory would change a poor man's life in an instant.

For the last twenty-four hours, Westbrook had been pondering why the elephant had breached the fence and gone missing in the first place. They had assumed he was in his final years—he was no longer having periods of musth, the dangerously aggressive sexual state that mature males go through annually, and his molars appeared to be his last of seven sets—so they assumed he would quietly pass on soon enough.

But instead he had crashed a heavy branch down onto the top of a thousand-volt electrified fence, short-circuiting it, then ripped one of the fence posts from the ground and simply walked out.

Why was he heading north? And what was he looking for so far away? He had come from somewhere in east Africa before his journey across the sea, Westbrook knew that much—but he didn't have any names or places yet.

His assistant, Rebecca Gaines, a sunny, soft-featured graduate student in veterinary medicine from San Diego State University—and like Westbrook more comfortable dealing with male animals than with men—was versed in tracking animal histories, so he figured she'd have names and locations by the time they had the bull in hand. It never occurred to him to ask his benefactor.

The sun was blinding as it rose over the hills to the east. The GPS locator on his laptop had lost the elephant's signal in the last few miles—due to the industrial-strength haze clinging to the hills, he surmised—

so they almost missed spotting the second helicopter hovering 500 feet below them as they sped past.

The pilot spoke into his headset. "That's got to be our man. Don't understand why he hasn't responded."

"Try him again," answered Westbrook. "In the meantime, let's go down and get a visual."

They banked and descended through the haze, and saw that the Eurocopter was stationed above a riverbed skirting a suburb of what was presumably Kabwe. One of the two rangers, who were twin brothers of the Luo tribe, pointed: Below an overpass that was clogged with cars and onlookers was the unmistakable shape of a large elephant standing in the shadows.

"Dat be our boy."

"What the hell's he doing?" shouted the pilot suddenly, and Westbrook's eyes were now drawn to the passenger side of the other helicopter, where a man was leaning out his open door with a high-powered rifle, unaware yet of the other helicopter's presence.

"Stop him!" yelled Westbrook, and his pilot quickly swung the bird around and brought it down not 100 feet from the second helicopter, stopping directly across from it. The gunman looked up in surprise, then with dawning comprehension as he saw the preserve's zebra-striped logo emblazoned on its side. He lifted his rifle and waved half-heartedly, then realized they were signaling for him to make radio contact.

"Damn it to hell. Put them through," Blackmon muttered into his mic, and his pilot switched the radio back on.

Once they were on the pre-arranged frequency, Blackmon and Westbrook began talking.

"Sorry for the communication snafu," Blackmon started. "Let's set down in the football field to our three o'clock and get this situation under control. Over."

"What's with the rifle, warden?" asked Westbrook pointedly as the two pilots began their descents. "He's no danger to anyone at his age."

"Oh, you'd be surprised how dangerous an old bull can be. I was just watching in case there was an incident. Like if some misguided fool got too close to him."

It sounded reasonable, but Westbrook had had an uneasy feeling about this game warden since they'd first spoken three days ago.

"We'll talk on the ground. Over."

By the time they had landed in the soccer field, the elephant had left the overpass with a throng of young men in pursuit, yelling and gesticulating. As they coolly shook hands, Blackmon shouted over the rotors' noise.

"As you can see, it's not an ideal situation."

Seeing Blackmon up close confirmed Westbrook's impression of him.

"No, but I want to avoid having to shoot him. Let me sedate him. Can you take care of the authorities?"

As Westbrook and his two rangers jogged in the direction the bull had taken, Blackmon stayed back momentarily to make a call to the local constabulary, asking for as many cars as they could spare for both crowd and traffic control. Westbrook took the opportunity to quickly instruct his rangers.

"I'm going to sedate him from the air. Stay with this guy, don't let him use his rifle under any circumstances. Understood?" They nodded their agreement and Westbrook turned and ran back towards his chopper, leaving Blackmon to the rangers.

The old bull was getting weaker and more despondent by the hour; there was only noxious-smelling water in the riverbed, and the trees were so thin and barren they offered no cover. And now he had the two-leggers to deal with.

They were chasing him fairly aggressively, but they had yet to do anything alarming. He had once again eluded the two-leggers' flying beast, but he knew it could come back any time it wanted to.

Perhaps this idea of his, this whole journey back to his birthplace, had been a mistake. Perhaps he should have stayed in his safe, familiar surroundings among his young male friends and just let them worship him until he laid down for the last time. It certainly would have been easier than this.

He saw now that the riverbed was blocked up ahead. A cascade of boulders had fallen from a nearby hillside and formed an impassable wall across the narrow bed. He swung around and started up the steep bank when he felt a sharp slap against his backside.

He looked around and saw a nearby two-legger throw another stone, this one glancing off his face just above his eye. Why would they do this, he wondered? It reminded him of the behavior some of the male two-leggers exhibited when he lived in the cold land where he had almost come to the end of his wits.

It was the same cruel, taunting behavior he had witnessed there, directed at him as well as at the other animals in the fenced enclosures. It always saddened him, this behavior, but physically it didn't really hurt, so he let it go. He just consigned it to the two-leggers' madness.

Westbrook quickly loaded the dart gun as his pilot took them back up. He needed just the right dose, because although this was a big bull he was also old and infirm, too much sedation could send him on a downward spiral.

He wanted the bull to lie down and pass out as opposed to collapsing, which could cut off circulation to a limb if one was inadvertently trapped beneath his massive weight.

And they would need to keep him in a twilight state until the preserve's transport truck arrived, which would hopefully be within the hour. It was all getting very complicated. Everything depended on the dose.

What he saw when they covered the ground to the beast made him see red: the fools were taunting the creature with stones! Westbrook saw his two rangers running at the young fools, waving frantically and probably screaming. The elephant had left the riverbed and was heading towards another overpass—but this time instead of going underneath it, he decided to cross the road. Where the hell were the police?

Several cars were already slowing as they saw the spectacle approaching, and then the giant creature was among them and several drivers panicked, backing away so quickly they collided with one another. Suddenly the warden had his rifle up and Westbrook realized he intended to use it. Then, to his everlasting relief and pride, his two rangers jumped in front of the warden, blocking a clean shot.

Westbrook considered what kind of dose it would take to knock a human out, and he would have done it, except now the elephant was crossing an open field and he realized it was the perfect place to dart him.

"All right," he spoke over his headset, "let's take him right here."

As they pursued him across the field and came in above and a little behind him, Westbrook shouldered the dart gun and took aim. It was not until that moment that he noticed the trail of blood running down from his left shoulder, and he realized right away this was no minor wound.

"What the hell...?" he wondered aloud, and now the pilot saw it too. To pierce an elephant's hide takes a major insult, and this one was deep. It was a wonder the bull was still on his feet.

"It's a bullet wound," the pilot observed as they hovered above him. "Doesn't look like it came from another elephant. Or a spear. Someone shot him."

Westbrook shouldered the gun again and fired the dart into the elephant's rump.

He reloaded as they pulled up and followed from a distance. They would trail him for a minute, and fire another dart if the first one hadn't taken effect. The bull seemed not to have even noticed the impact. He just kept lumbering on across the field, trying to escape the helicopter.

Then he slowed and listed to one side, and a few seconds later he came to a woozy halt. Then he sat down on his haunches and stared up at the chopper, and Westbrook realized he couldn't really see it anymore.

Within seconds he was laying on his side, and the helicopter landed and Westbrook ran to the beast as his rangers joined him.

Westbrook had brought his full veterinary kit, and he was thankful he had: the surgery to remove the bullet—it was mushroomed and intact—required laboring through two feet of necrotic flesh and sewing up the wound with a dissolvable anti-bacterial packing left inside.

They had stationed Blackmon at the edge of the field to keep the crowd at a distance until the police arrived, so Westbrook couldn't see the expression on Blackmon's face as he watched them work.

Blackmon had seen the wound as they all ran to the downed bull, and he realized with growing certainty that this had been the result of his firing the Rigby in frustration. They would find that the bullet had been fired from a large calibre rifle, from above, and they would doubtless come looking for an explanation. He wasn't usually the dishonest type, he told himself, but he obviously had to deny it.

By then the preserve's truck had arrived with a crew of young acolytes who Blackmon begrudgingly waved through. He granted short interviews to the two television news crews, whom he ordered the police to hold back along with the crowd while the elephant was treated and then carefully hoisted into the truck's open trailer by its crane.

They were about to administer the sedation's antidote and close up the trailer when Rebecca approached Westbrook with the results of her search; she had her MacBook open and a look of wonderment on her face as she stared in at the sleeping giant.

He was no garden-variety African elephant, she explained: this male had traveled the world and then been brought back to Africa twelve years ago, but not to his original home. He had been born in Tsavo National Park some fifty years ago.

She traced the path he had taken so far on a Google map for Westbrook: it was a virtually straight line northeast from the preserve, and if followed seven hundred miles further, it ran straight to Tsavo. He was apparently going back to what he considered his birthplace, and he had an uncanny sense of direction to guide him, so the odds of his finding the Kenyan park, if he survived the journey, were probably excellent.

Westbrook could hear the admiration in her voice, and he too felt a strange kinship with the creature as he stared in at its massive head and tusks, its kind eyes open but unseeing.

For years Westbrook had heard stories of the species' capacity for emotion and their profound sentience, and he had observed some of it, but if Rebecca's theory was correct, this journey was an order of magnitude beyond anything he had considered. Decades after being taken from his home, then dropped over a thousand miles away in a landscape he had never seen, this creature's intelligence and heart were so powerful that they were guiding him home? Unbelievable.

* * *

Werner Brandeis stood at his floor to ceiling windows as the streetlights came on across Central Park sixty floors below, listening on speakerphone as the three arguments were proposed by the different parties.

Even though it meant losing custody of the elephant, he quickly agreed to eliminate the first option, which was to return the bull to his preserve. It was now clear that the elephant would just smash down the fence again and start his trek over. He wanted to go home, and there was not much they could do to stop this instinct, even if they were of a mind to. Which they weren't.

The second option, proposed by the Zambian authorities, was to leave him in the transport and take him all the way to Tsavo National Park and release him there. This way they would eliminate three to four weeks of possible disasters, both to the elephant and the populations of two more countries he would have to pass through. Expedite his trek, avoid a lot of wear and tear on everyone. It seemed like a no-brainer.

But there was a third option which was gaining traction, and it appealed to Brandeis' difficult, outlier nature. It would cost quite a bit of money, but Brandeis could afford to underwrite it. It was poetic, it was a grand gesture, and the media could be influenced to spin it as a great, heartwarming story. It had a lot of moving parts, any of which could go off the rails, but Brandeis was brilliant at selling this kind of complex campaign.

Once again, his world-famous fortune was so influential that even high government officials in three countries were cowed by it. In the end, no one could say no to Werner Brandeis and his money.

The elephant regained consciousness that night with a large headache, a dull pain in his shoulder, and the strange sensation that there was more to the surrounding darkness than the silent, empty field he found himself in.

Chapter Eleven

Kenya 1968-1969

THE MORNING CAN DAWN *perfectly peaceful, your stomach full and your family content and loving beside you, and by that night your body can be alone on a riverbank, the birds of death picking at your flesh and the light gone from your eyes.*

The earth we walk upon has no memory of us; its only concern is the constancy of day into night, season after season, and the memory of any one of us is soon gone from the earth forever.

This gives me a great sadness when I dwell upon it, so I store every pleasing moment I experience so that I may visit them when the sadness becomes overwhelming. You might see me standing in front of you, perhaps eating from a flame tree, and think that I am really there, but I am not. I am in my memory, perhaps years away from the place where I appear to be standing.

The end of my days with my two-legger family came that next rainy season when Mother Blue and her clan returned for me as they had promised. The kind young two-legger who had been my closest friend during that period followed me for a time, and the herd became so used to him that he would travel in our midst during the day and sleep by a small fire at night, watched over by us. Eventually he said his goodbyes to me and returned to his home.

From time to time other members of my two-legger family would visit me, and it was always highly emotional for both of us. My herd mates were not overly friendly with them, but they never threatened their false beasts, even when they came close enough to touch. Mother Blue made a rule that no infant be allowed to play with the two-leggers, lest they lose their distrust of them. That could spell death for an elephant.

The next period, as I grew into male-hood and started gaining my independence, was the most exhilarating of my life so far, though at the time I didn't realize it would not last; I thought life would always keep getting fuller. I watch my young male friends now as they go through the same foolishness, but I know to let them discover the truth in their own time.

I began to understand the more complicated rules of behavior, and the ways of the herd took on new meaning as I became a full member, which meant I was willing to give my life for the clan if called upon. I settled into the rhythms and gradual changes that overtake us all. My body grew to twice its size in barely more than three seasons, and I soon was the largest young bull in the clan. My tusks began to grow out, and my aunties all said they were well-formed and would be extremely large, which would serve me well as an adult.

Except for the bulls who were about to go off to join a bachelor herd, I was the strongest, most powerful male in the clan, and I could vanquish any of my peers in our matches with either brute strength or force of will. I was a proud, desirable specimen; little did I know then that it could eventually be my undoing.

* * *

The changes Gichinga had warned Russell of swept through east Africa like a dark wind, at least as far as white British society was concerned. There were still safaris to be run by the big companies, since they provided hundreds of jobs and millions of dollars in income, but the sea change was obvious to everyone: The native Africans were on the ascent, and even though there were tribal rivalries that crippled their rise, the government was now firmly in African hands, and the wealthy, formerly powerful whites who didn't flee to Europe or South Africa had to answer to "under-educated" black bureaucrats who could tie up a simple transaction for months if the proper attitude was not displayed—or, more aptly, if the proper bribe was not proffered.

Russell and the other white hunters soon realized they alone could not stop the poaching epidemic that was decimating the elephant and rhino populations, nor could Rupert Matthews and his friends; the corruption was just too endemic, and the area that had to be covered was too vast.

So Russell and his friends recruited several dozen teams of rangers from the fierce nomadic tribes. They called them the Field Force; armed with rifles and outfitted with radios, the Field Force would roam the parks in pairs with orders to engage the poachers, sometimes even shooting to kill if necessary.

Paid from the profits of the safari companies as well as by the Kenyatta regime, which had to appear to be anti-poaching, the Field Force put a major dent in the slaughter, but there were still thousands of elephants butchered every year. Ivory was too valuable to the middlemen selling to the Asian market; none of them understood, or cared, that these animals felt great pain and loss.

And the Asians themselves were even more oblivious; the Filipino Catholic church was, and is, the biggest buyer of illicit ivory carvings in the world. And in the case of the worst offender, the Chinese, the government assures their people that no elephants are killed when cutting off their tusks. The tusks simply grow back once they've been "harvested."

After his initial experience enforcing the anti-poaching plan, Russell, for one, was happy to turn the job over to the Field Force. Though he was fearless when it came to hunting in the most dangerous of settings, having to risk daily skirmishes with poachers was not in the plans of a middle-aged family man anymore.

And there were more changes afoot in Russell's life. The kind, as he told himself later in a reflective moment, that always arrive when you least expect them.

* * *

Jean had fallen for Russell when she'd met him at a party at the Swiss embassy in London in the spring of 1948. He was so dashing he could have been a movie star, so when she found he was from a good upper-class family and had been a decorated officer in the war, she decided not to hold his looks against him.

After an intense courtship and then a formal engagement, he asked her family if he could take her on a trip to East Africa, and as she drove with him out of Nairobi and they left the road a few miles later, he asked her to close her eyes until they crested a rise.

When he told her to open them again, she looked out at an expanse of lush savanna rolling away for miles, with countless herds dotting the plains under a sky stacked with thunderheads, and it was all over. Like Russell when he had first beheld the majesty of untamed Africa, she knew that she had come home.

Jean accompanied Russell on safaris when there was a family booking—as opposed to just a stag outing—so that the client's wife, if she wasn't a hunter, would have someone to talk with. They would take a second vehicle which would be photographic-only, driven by a second white hunter. They would split up the park's territory so that neither car would be within miles of the other until they met back in camp.

That summer of 1968, a famous Hollywood producer, Jack Singer, and his new wife, a film actress thirteen years his junior, had brought along two teenaged sons from Singer's first marriage, ostensibly to teach them how to become "men" by shooting as many of the Big Five as possible. Father and sons had bagged three lions between them so far, as well as two leopards, two cape buffalo and a rhino. But they hadn't had any luck spotting a trophy-sized elephant, and the father was obsessed with bringing one down before he had to return to America.

Then one evening on their way back to camp—two days before the safari was to end—Kagwe whistled from his spotter's perch and pointed at a lone bull standing on a distant hillside. His tusks, in the brief moment they saw him before he disappeared into a wall of brush, were world class. He was obviously a wily old bull to have survived this long, so Russell knew immediately this would be a challenging hunt.

The light was fading fast. Russell realized they might not be able to find him in the morning if they came back; even following his spoor, this bull could put ten miles on them if he felt spooked, and this one had probably seen everything in his time.

So Russell steered toward where the bull had disappeared, and asked Singer if he was comfortable going into the bush after him.

"It might get a bit hairy in there, are you up for it? He's bloody huge."

"How much light do we have?" Singer's throat was tight from sudden nerves, but he was trying not to show it. He wasn't a particularly good hunter—his older son was a better shot with more nerve—but he was paying a fortune to be here, and white hunters are all about making the client feel important.

"Maybe ten minutes. We're going to have to get a bit lucky."

They reached the spot where the bull had gone in. Russell and Kagwe jumped out and listened, then heard the crashing of the bull deep in the brush.

The gun bearer handed Singer his rifle, but stayed behind with Singer's younger son; it was deemed too dangerous for anyone but Russell, Kagwe and the client to go in. The second car was probably back in camp by now, the ladies being served cocktails in the lantern-lit dining tent.

They entered the brush, which was thorn-covered and eight to ten feet high, with a network of tunnels and small clearings carved into it over the years by myriad game.

The visibility was sketchy, and the tunnels were serpentine, so they had to round each bend with great caution. It was not a place most humans would choose to be; on their turf, close up, elephants are the most dangerous game in the world. They charge when threatened, and if a big rifle is not fatal on the first or second shot, they will grab the tormentor with their trunk and slam him into the ground, perhaps impale him with one of their tusks, or simply crush him under 10,000 pounds of seething muscle.

But this was why Russell was such a sought-after hunter; he relished these encounters, and the royalty of Europe and America got their thrills following him into harm's way and living to tell about it.

Russell and Kagwe led Singer up several passageways, using hand signals they'd perfected over years. They had gone maybe 100 yards when the sounds—and the strangely sweet scent—of elephants was suddenly overwhelming. Russell stopped, his hand up.

He and Kagwe realized that there wasn't just the one bull—there were several elephants in the brush all around them. Russell looked into Singer's eyes and saw that he too realized this, and he was petrified.

To be in the brush with a panicked client holding a loaded rifle was almost as dangerous as being surrounded by elephants, so Russell signaled that they should turn around and go back the way they'd come.

They were half way to the opening when the brush forty feet in front of them burst outward, and there stood a mature elephant blocking their exit. It was not the bull with the big ivory; it was a cow, but in the close quarters she seemed immense.

The three of them froze, hoping she might not see them, but it was too late for that. She had smelled them, and when she swung her head around and spotted them, Russell saw the murderous look in her eyes and quickly brought his rifle up. So did Singer.

She charged, and would have been on them in three quick strides had not both rifles opened up with deafening blasts, and the cow tumbled to the earth literally inches from their feet. With that, the brush around them exploded with noise as the rest of the herd took off.

In the ensuing silence, Kagwe picked himself up from the ground where he had taken cover—he carried no rifle—and inspected the dead cow. Russell looked at Singer, who was just getting his breath back.

"Nice shooting," Russell said softly, and Singer flushed with pride. "We'll come back in the morning, see if we can find the bull's tracks, but it's going to be a long shot."

A sudden rustling in the brush nearby made them all whirl, and then a heartbreaking sight materialized from the shadows. A baby elephant walked tentatively up to them, its tiny trunk sniffing at the cow's lifeless face. Then it raised its trunk in the air and sniffed at the humans and let out a confused, pitiful whimper.

Russell knelt and stroked the two-month-old calf, his head lowered in anguish.

"It's why she charged us. We must have gotten between her and her calf." Russell sighed and chambered another round. "He won't last long out here, and he doesn't deserve that kind of death."

"God no, you can't kill him! Jean rescues orphans, right?"

"He's way too young. No one's ever raised a calf at this age."

Singer couldn't take his eyes off the little elephant, who was now climbing onto his mother's corpse trying to wake her.

"Well, we can try. Whatever it takes, I'll cover it."

In that moment Russell's opinion of Jack Singer made a 180 degree turn.

"You OK with letting the bull go then? If we rescue this guy, we won't have any time…"

"Forget about the bull. I don't want to do any more shooting."

Russell slid the safety back on and slung his rifle over his shoulder. He spoke briefly to Kagwe in Kikuyu, who hurried off toward the Land Rover.

Jean and several of her "boys" were caring for the baby elephant that first night, and after Russell watched the Singer family retire to their tents for bed, he made his way to the pen the boys had fashioned for the little orphan.

Jean gave a look to her helpers and they quietly slipped out of the enclosure, leaving husband and wife alone with the sleeping calf. His breathing was long and steady in the darkness, his tummy full of Jean's new formula.

Russell sat down on the blanket beside her and said simply, "I'm desperately sorry. I know there are no excuses for this…"

There was a resigned look in her eyes that was almost worse than anger. There is a moment in most failed marriages that, if acknowledged and dealt with, can possibly save the relationship. If missed, there is no going back. Russell realized he was on the brink of that moment, and the certainty of this made his heart cold with fear.

"You have a choice to make, Russell. Not whether you and I can go on like this, because we can't." She let this hang in the air for a moment before continuing. "It's whether you want to stay stuck in the past…or be part of the future. The change is already here, but you keep your head buried in the sand."

"I know," Russell said softly. "And I agree. This was the last straw."

"You could be one of the most persuasive examples of the new way. To have Russell Hathaway, world-renowned big game hunter, give up hunting and go photographic-only? That would be gigantic in my world."

Russell nodded. He had heard her entreaties for years, but like the alcoholic who hasn't hit bottom yet, it took this sad turn of events to finally convince him that the path he was on was the wrong one. If he lost his old clients—and the money they brought in—so be it. At least this would go a long way towards saving his marriage.

He was ready to make the change.

CHAPTER TWELVE

Kenya, 1969-1970

IN FACT, JEAN HAD ALREADY begun to make changes that would have repercussions for the two of them, as well as for all wildlife in East Africa. She used her orphanage, which, along with her name, was becoming well-known in preservationist circles and beyond, to back several pro-wildlife initiatives as well as helping groom sympathetic Kenyans to run for office.

She became a gentle force in progressive Nairobi political circles, and was always a sight to behold in the halls of government, an elegant beauty with an orphaned baby chimp or lemur perched on her shoulder. Their charm and innocence was almost always successful in getting recalcitrant ministers or bureaucrats to at least sit down and have a conversation.

Her greatest accomplishment, in her mind, was to have raised three unique, loving humans. Even though her own two would leave Africa behind, she would always have Kamau, whom she knew would never leave. He may not have been blood, but she felt as close to him as to her own children. And her children and Kamau were as close as any siblings could be.

After she and Russell had seen to his schooling while he was living with them at Salisbury, he was admitted to the University of Nairobi for the fall of 1970 with a full scholarship to study veterinary medicine.

It had been three years since Ishi had left with his adoptive herd, and after the humans felt sure he was acclimated, they had let go of him, if not the memory of him. Russell would spot him every now and then when his herd passed through the park, and their reunions were always emotional for both of them. Russell's clients were allowed to interact with him through the Land Rover's windows, where his trunk would explore their faces amidst delighted laughter. One look in his gentle, soulful eyes, and they invariably came away moved.

These photographic-only clients were very different from the hunting crowd—sweet, deluded tree-huggers, if Russell had to be blunt about it—but that was OK. He didn't miss the heavy drinking and smoking that invariably came with the guns. And now, with the changing times, big game hunters had started to become marginalized, and the number of hunting safaris was way down. Russell realized he had made a propitious—if not entirely voluntary—decision to forego hunting.

* * *

Even though he had been raised in a "civilized" environment for the last several years, there was still a bit of the wild in Kamau. When his best friend from his village, Ndegwa, would show up at Salisbury from time to time, they would go off on walkabouts, armed only with bows and arrows or spears, and live by their wits. It kept Kamau in touch with the Kikuyu warrior still inside him, and even though he was too educated to believe in the old tribal ways, the hormones of an eighteen-year old male are impossible to dismiss.

That August before Kamau was to leave for university, Ndegwa arrived for what they both knew might be their last adventure together. Ndegwa was the village chief's first-born son, so they both had paths laid out for them that would take their lives in completely different directions. As melancholy as that realization made them, they knew they would be friends for life, so they set out on this journey as if nothing would ever change between them.

The rains that season had left the plains lush and overgrown. The herbivores had the best vegetation to graze in years, and the carnivores had the best hunting in their lifetimes. It was in that fat, easy environment that the two friends hunted and talked for the last time as young men.

* * *

Gichinga Kimathi had come up in the world. After abandoning his wife and their child in Eldama Ravine, he had moved to the bustling township of Voi, where he worked for the new government as a debt collector.

He had avoided Tsavo for the last few years, partially because of his brush with Russell, but mostly because of the advent of the Field Force. Now there was so much demand for ivory from the buyers in Nairobi and Mombasa, at five times the old price, that his former trade became too lucrative to forgo.

He found a new crew and began to go out on the occasional weekend. East and West Tsavo are spread over 6,000 square miles, and except for the lone railroad tracks and a dirt "highway" running through the center of it, the park is virtually devoid of humans besides the rangers, the occasional safari, and a few small villages. If they were dropped off and later picked up by truck, Gichinga figured, they could make brief forays in and have a very low risk of being caught.

And if worse came to worse, they would draw down on the rangers. Rarely did the Field Force have more than two men, and his crew had five men armed with powerful rifles. There would be no rangers crazy enough to confront them.

At eighteen, Ndegwa was a highly skilled hunter and tracker, and there was little he ever missed with his nose or his ears. So as he and Kamau roasted a dik dik over a fire outside a cave hidden in an ancient lava field they had frequented many times before, Ndegwa clicked a signal to Kamau and nodded to the west.

In the setting sun Kamau couldn't see anything, but the birds had just fallen silent and Ndegwa had smelled it. Humans, close by and coming this way.

The boys silently withdrew to the mouth of the cave and watched as five armed men in non-tribal garb walked into the lava field. The group's leader—Kamau and Ndegwa could tell by his and his crew's interactions that he was the dominant male—looked around the field to see who had made the fire, and quietly gave orders to find them.

A bolt of adrenaline shot through Kamau when he saw the leader's face in the gloaming. It was the first time he'd laid eyes on him since the slaughter six years ago, but Gichinga had not changed much.

Kamau whispered to Ndegwa. "We are in grave danger. That man is from our village, do you remember him?"

"Yes, it is Gichinga Kimathi from years ago," whispered Ndegwa. "My father was one of the elders that forced him to leave." He thought about it for a moment and then made a decision.

"Show no fear. Act as if we've never seen him before."

Ndegwa stepped out into the light of the fire, his hands open in welcome. Then Kamau joined him, and the two looked innocently at the poachers, as if there should be nothing to fear.

"Good evening, fellow hunters. Would you like to join us at our fire?"

The poachers looked to their leader for guidance, and Gichinga smiled coolly.

"Ah, and good evening to you as well, my young friends. You are very kind." He stared into each of their eyes, looking for recognition of any kind. They gave none back, so Gichinga continued. "We didn't expect to find anyone out here. Are you from a nearby village?"

"No sir, our village is a three day walk to the north," answered Ndegwa with conviction. "Near Lake Nyeri, if you know it."

"Ah, yes, I used to...I grew up in these parts," Gichinga answered and then stopped, catching himself. "Well, please allow us to spread our blankets for the night. We have our own food, but you are most kind."

The poachers had by now all lowered their weapons, accepting the innocence of these boy-men. After all, they'd been raised in similar villages in much the same way. They'd all been sweet and innocent once, and had all been on walkabouts in their youth.

By the time the poachers were ready to retire they'd polished off three bottles of rum that could have powered a car. The men climbed under their blankets and passed out one by one, leaving the boys to their fire.

If they had a stash of freshly killed elephants' tusks buried somewhere they certainly didn't divulge it. Gichinga had probably warned them what to do and say; for instance, he was adamant that the fire be put out before the boys went to sleep. He was apparently more concerned with rangers spotting the glow then predators walking amongst them.

As the boys retreated to the cave and laid out their blankets, Ndegwa whispered to Kamau.

"We should be gone by first light."

"No," answered Kamau. "We should be gone immediately. I trust walking among lions more than I trust sleeping next to that man. I don't want to wake up with a machete slashing my throat."

The young men reached the highway just before dawn and flagged down the first vehicle that passed, which happened to be a van filled with lavatory fittings for apartments in Nairobi. The driver, an Indian tradesman, was suspicious at first until Kamau spoke to him in perfect English, whereupon he agreed to take them to the nearest guard gate.

There, Kamau was able to use the radio to call the warden, who dispatched a dozen members of the Field Force to the lava field with orders to be ready for a possibly violent confrontation.

While Kamau and Ndegwa hitched a ride back to the turnoff for their village, the Field Force arrived to find the ashes of a cooking fire and discarded bottles of rum, but the poachers long gone. When the poachers had been roused by Gichinga before dawn to eliminate the witnesses to their presence, they'd found an empty cave and realized they had been outwitted, and they took off, knowing that the boys would likely alert the authorities.

Even though he'd suspected Gichinga of slitting their throats, Kamau never knew how close he'd actually come to bleeding out in a cave.

CHAPTER THIRTEEN

London, New York and Kenya 1970-1972

ADOLESCENCE IS HARD enough when you're straight: add having to live in the closet, in provincial Nairobi, and it becomes unbearable. Terence had had longings for his best friend at Bedford, but since the friend was straight, there was nothing he could do to experiment, and he knew that to ask anyone about his feelings would bring shame and humiliation.

The summer after his graduation, Terence got a job working in a London art gallery for a friend of his father's. His face had healed from the "accident," though his speech was subtly affected and the psychological scars would never disappear completely. In his senior year he'd shot up several inches and turned from a soft, spoiled, lost boy into a gorgeous, lean young man—albeit still confused. He had no idea the looks he got from people he passed on the street, but with his new wardrobe of tight bell bottoms, bohemian coats and wavy hair flowing to his shoulders, he was soon hanging out in the coolest clubs in Swinging London.

It was not until his first kiss with a man that he realized why he'd felt such an emptiness, and a lack of attraction to girls, all his adolescent years. He dove headlong into this new world, and as he met the cream of London's gay scene, he tried to make up for lost time.

He was smitten with the music swirling around Britain—David Bowie and Glam Rock were in ascendance at the time—so he took up singing again, something he'd loved as a kid. Unfortunately, he'd never learned to read music, and he didn't have a gift for lyrics, so the bands he auditioned for chose more experienced musicians over his arresting look. But it did get him onto the periphery of the music world, where he talked his way into being a photographer's assistant shooting stills for album covers.

He soon was making enough money to afford sharing an apartment with three other new arrivals, all of them young, smart and pretty, and he wrote his parents that he had applied to the University of London with the intent of majoring in design. He was sorry to leave his home behind, he wrote, but, like his sister, he had chosen to live abroad for the foreseeable future.

For her part, Amanda had followed her new calling and been accepted at Columbia University, the most prestigious journalism school in the world at the time, and as she walked the streets of the Village and the Upper West Side, drinking in the music, the sights and smells wafting from apartment windows and storefronts and parks, she could read in the faces of her fellow travelers that this was all part of the sea change she had foreseen.

Little did she, or any of them, know that the counter culture would be over in a scant few years; that most of the world, including the silent majorities of the great metropolis', could not care less.

At the end of the day, the movement was absorbed by the corporate world and used to sell products. The civil rights and Vietnam War protests died out by the mid 1970s, and almost everything besides music, sexual habits and drug use went back to normal. No matter how much the Boomer Generation—or at least a vocal minority of it—wanted to believe otherwise, human nature never really changes, at least not for long.

* * *

As wet as the rainy seasons had been for the last few years, the law of averages caught up with the game on the east African plains in 1972 with a vengeance. The dry season lasted far longer than it had in any of the herd's memories, and though they knew to seek out the cooler highlands, even there the grasses were parched and the trees bone dry.

The plains animals began to die off by the thousands, and then so did some of the elephants, the older, weaker females first, whose weight dropping precipitously until they didn't have enough stamina to keep up with the herd.

For a young bull like Ishi—he was ten now, in the prime of adolescence—this was the first he'd ever experienced such a long drought, and, forced into a diet of thistles and sips of dirty, sandy water, he too began to drop weight.

All of their hides were hanging in folds, their stores of fat going or gone. Several of his favorite old aunties succumbed, and in his famished torpor, Ishi's heart ached until he didn't think he could go on. But in the end, he went on, along with the rest of the grieving herd. They would be back to bury their friends' bones in the rainy season.

But first they had to survive the wildfires, a once-in-a-generation succession of infernos that devastated east Africa that year.

The lightning strikes were far enough away that the sea of emaciated plains-dwellers barely noticed at first. The hope was that the clouds would bring rain, but all they brought was more heat—and an ethereal evening wind. Then the sky crackled and boomed, and the clouds sizzled with electricity. The scent of ozone was thick in the air.

Suddenly the elephants smelled the bad thing. They looked to the east, where a cloud much darker then the sky had turned the sun blood red.

Then the earth rumbled as the first wave of animals fleeing from the east crested a rise, coming this way. Just before they reached the herd and stormed through them, a wall of insects swept past, the lowest-flying ones slamming into the herd's eyes, temporarily blinding them.

Before he knew it, Ishi was cut off from his clan as the plains-dwellers took everything along with them like a tsunami.

Several members of the clan never heard the entreaties of Mother Blue or the other females over the pounding hooves, and the herd was divided and swept in several different directions by the sheer force of the stampede.

I found myself alone in a copse of trees and let the other animals thunder past. I looked around but saw no sign of my herd. In fact, now there were only smaller animals skittering in panic, snakes and rodents searching desperately for a friendly hole to hide in. The last of the tree dwellers hit the ground and, chatterless for once, ran for their lives. Even the birds had flown.

I called out to my clan again. Nothing came back but the dust silently settling from the receding masses' fury. I felt a familiar coldness creeping up in the pit of my stomach, and realized it was because I was now completely alone; there was no help coming. I was almost a mature bull now, and I was going to have to survive this on my own.

Suddenly a burning ember landed in the trees next to me and flames erupted. More embers rained down, and small fires began breaking out everywhere I looked. I started running and dodging, looking for a place to hide, but there was nothing.

I turned and saw the swirling orange wall approaching, perhaps a minute away, and it stretched across the entire horizon. It even had a voice, I imagined in my panic, and it was a fearsome, angry wail. Then a pall of smoke descended all around me, and I could barely see.

I ran, choking and gasping, as fast as my legs would take me. Soon I was heading down a steep hill, whereupon the smoke lifted.

The savanna that appeared ahead of me was littered with dying, thrashing plains-dwellers who had fallen and been trampled. Some were dragging their broken bodies by their front legs, a sight that made me even more distraught, which made me run even faster.

When I could run no further, I stopped to gather my breath, and as I looked around, my heart pounding, I thought I saw one of my herd standing at the base of an escarpment, hidden by shadows and a cascade of giant boulders its same dark color. But why was he or she not calling to me, I wondered?

I approached, and then saw that this was no member of my clan, but an enormous old bull with huge tusks and an attitude that simmered with disdain. I had seen him before, at the rainy season gatherings where mature males were welcomed for a few weeks. His name was Big Black, and he was known as one of the most difficult, angry bulls in our world.

"Big Black, sir," I called, "we haven't met formally, but I certainly know of you by reputation. If you know of a place to hide, I would be most grateful."

As I got closer, I saw streams of fluid leaking from his temples, a sign of arousal in mature males. This did not augur well for his mood, but at this point, I didn't much care. I wanted an old bull's tricks to save me from certain death.

Big Black rumbled, "What is your name and what clan are you from?"

This was hardly the time for a conversation, but I answered, hoping to befriend him.

"I was born into the clan of Red Eye, and when she passed on, my mother became leader. Moon Mother. They were all killed by two-leggers, and I was adopted by the clan of Mother Blue."

Big Black seemed to be trying to remember these names from the hundreds of clans he must have come across in his lifetime; then he shook his massive head.

"You had the misfortune of being raised with one of the most miserable cows I have ever known. She Storms. Dreadful, truly dreadful."

His memory was intact, but I got the impression that something wasn't quite right with him.

"I'll tell you a story about her if you'd like," I offered. "While we wait this out, perhaps?"

"And have you already been cast out, boy? You look abandoned, if I might say so." He pulled up a clump of grass, knocked the dirt off against a knee, and stuffed it in his mouth.

I looked over my shoulder and saw the flaming wall raging only a few hundred feet away. Then the heat started to hit us. Big Black seemed to hardly notice.

"No, I have not been cast out yet, sir, but I have lost my clan for the moment and I am getting very nervous. Are you planning to wait it out right here, or do you have somewhere else in mind?"

I heard another bull's voice call petulantly from somewhere behind Big Black.

"Who are you talking to? Let's get inside before it's too late!"

Big Black turned and glared at the miscreant, a young bull slightly older than me.

"Don't piddle yourself. If you need to, you go on inside. I'm greeting a new member of our little clan here. He's been abandoned by his aunties." He turned and looked at me quizzically. "I don't remember—did you tell me your name?"

"I must have forgotten to, sir. It's Ishi. I'll explain that too, but I think we must be getting 'inside' right away." Embers had started to rain down, and the hot, toxic smoke was roiling towards us.

Big Black sighed and shambled away into the boulders.

"Come with me, boy. You'll be safe with us."

I followed a winding path through the boulders that ended at the base of the escarpment. And there I saw five other young bulls waiting anxiously, varying in age from ten to twenty or thereabouts. They all turned now and walked into a subterranean opening, which I realized was the entrance to a cave.

As my eyes adjusted to the darkness, I saw that there were scores of other plains-dwellers milling about in a cool, cavernous chamber. They moved aside as we made our way in and walked to the farthest wall. There we turned and faced the entrance expectantly.

A moment later the light outside turned brilliantly orange and we all heard the roar and hiss of the malevolence as it passed over our hiding place. No one made a sound.

And so began a new, unexpected period of my life. I had always known that males were asked to leave the clan once they could mount a female; I had certainly witnessed it. It is the most traumatic event in a young bull's life. So it was no surprise that this little bachelor herd was a collection of bitter, lost males following a demented old bull in order to have company and protection in a lonely, dangerous world.

I decided to stay with them for the time being; I could travel with them until I found signs of my clan.

It was nightfall before we ventured outside. As we walked upon the charred earth, there were patches of glowing red amidst the blackness, and a pungent, acrid smell. I realized we would have to travel for several days to find forage, and any scent of my clan would be erased by then. I would have to scent for their droppings once we reached unburnt land, and then hope I would be wise enough to follow the path Mother Blue would have taken. Otherwise I might not see them again for many seasons—if ever. The thought of this made it hard to breathe. Would I be left behind again?

As the sun came up on the desolate landscape, I realized that one of the young bulls had been an old playmate of mine from my youth. It was thrilling to have someone who knew me from back then, but it was also somewhat awkward: he had been part of She Storms's family, and had gone with her clan when she was banished. We had been good friends until that awful day, and he admitted that She Storms was certainly capable of the accusation, so we soon got over our distress. His name was now Little Stream. This because he couldn't stop his urine from constantly dribbling as he walked. He had a nice pair of tusks for his age, even bigger than mine, but I could harbor no jealousy towards such a kind soul.

His extended family had been fortunate to survive intact; their tragedies were of the usual variety, loved ones dying from time to time, but nothing cataclysmic. She Storms had taken them to the land below the great snow-crowned mountain, and they had prospered there. But She Storms lasted only one rainy season as matriarch; she was killed by the arrow of a two-legger barely bigger than a child, and her agony over the days it took for her to die was apparently terrible. Even I was moved upon hearing of her suffering.

Little Stream had heard of my clan's end, and he was quite emotional when he realized I had survived; the other clans assumed that our entire herd had been reduced to bones, yet here I was.

By this time I was getting to know the other bachelors a bit, though none of them were very friendly yet, and Big Black was keeping to himself as he led us toward the faint outline of unburnt hills looming a few days away.

I told Little Stream of losing my adoptive clan, and that I hoped to track them and rejoin them. He fell strangely silent. So did the other young bulls. They all seemed to be wary of Big Black's temper; he now stopped and turned toward me.

"Search for your clan, will you? The ones who abandoned you in the face of death yesterday, and who will assuredly abandon you again the day you get a little too mature for their liking? That clan?"

There was a chorus of agreement and trunk swinging among the other bachelors, and then Big Black walked on. I felt small and foolish.

"You're perhaps a season or two away from being cast out, you know," spoke Little Stream quietly. "I know. I'm a season older than you, and my own mother won't even speak to me." He stood there, urine trickling down his hind legs. "Maybe it was meant to be—them leaving you behind, and then you finding us. Maybe it was a sign."

"They did not leave me behind!" I bellowed. I closed my eyes in anguish, torn by my love for my clan...and an unacknowledged feeling that my time

was definitely coming. Mother Blue and the other females weren't even my blood. Why would they make an exception of me?

I had seen other males my age hanging on to their clans for weeks, skulking pitifully on the edges, coldly ignored by their mothers, their aunties, even their male playmates whose time had not yet come. And then one morning they were gone. It was not a place I ever wanted to be.

Perhaps what Little Stream had said was true. Perhaps this had been a sign…and I had been sleepwalking through the reality of what was coming. Perhaps the best thing to do was travel with this clan and make the transition to adulthood, and avoid the heartbreak of tracking my clan down—only to find out that I was not welcomed back.

Yes, I thought, this might be the way. I would grieve for my lost clan as I traveled with the bachelor herd. But more—and I did not realize this yet—I would grieve for my lost youth.

CHAPTER FOURTEEN

Tanzania, London and Manhattan, Present Day

THE MEDIA HAD FALLEN hard for Brandeis' idea, as he'd predicted. How could they pass up such a feel-good story—following an old bull elephant as he trekked a thousand miles through unknown territory and untold dangers trying to find his way back home...so he could die? It was tragic, it was suspenseful, and it would play out over roughly four weeks. It was great reality television. Once the story got out, Brandeis figured it would be carried around the globe.

It would be well worth his expenditures on the advance teams who were clearing any obstacles in the elephant's path, on the scouts paralleling him to prevent anyone from doing him harm, and on the payoffs to each of the countries' governments as the circus passed through their territory.

All this was going on at least a mile from their subject, who was never supposed to be aware that he was being monitored, subtly guided, and beamed around the globe from cameras hidden in trees or on helicopters 2,000 feet aloft. It would not only bring in millions of dollars to wildlife organizations everywhere, it would help transform the public's perception of the plight of wild animals in a fast-shrinking world.

All of this brilliance, of course, depending on things going according to plan.

The last thirty miles to the Zambia/Tanzania border—and the border crossing itself—was going to be problematic, thought Westbrook as he collapsed onto his rented motor home's bed for the first full night's sleep he'd had in days. But from there the journey would likely get easier: most of the remaining six hundred miles across Tanzania to the Kenyan border went through national parks and lake regions, not populated areas that required stopping traffic and controlling human interactions.

The only hitch to their plans was that the elephant preferred traveling at night. Around midday he would find a shaded spot to lay up in, then hit the road again when the light fell, which meant they had a lot of time to kill.

That led them to the most vital questions of all, and the answers would hopefully fill in everything. First, besides ostensibly wanting to return to his birthplace, was the elephant looking for his original birth herd? And second, he had been raised in Tsavo fifty years ago by humans; might they not still be alive? Westbrook put Rebecca on it, and she came back with several answers the next morning.

The family had been that of a famous white hunter, his wife, and their two children. Jean Hathaway had started one of the first animal orphanages in Africa around 1962, and was reputed to have been the first person to successfully raise a baby elephant and, several years later, release it in the wild. If that baby elephant was by some freak chance their bull, the story just got even better.

Rebecca had located Russell Hathaway, who was now an 87-year old landscape painter living outside of London, and one of the two children, the daughter, who had fortuitously re-taken her maiden name after a divorce, so she popped right up when Rebecca Googled her. Amanda Hathaway was now a noted 63-year old journalist and author also living in England. Jean and their son Terence had apparently passed away years ago. Rebecca promised more details to follow.

Brandeis would obviously want to fly the surviving family members down to Kenya to be there for the bull's arrival. If the bull recognized them after all these years, there wouldn't be a dry eye in the house. If they could get all the pieces to fall into place, Westbrook figured as he dialed Brandeis in New York, it was going to be a heartbreaker. And he was pretty certain it was all going to fall into place, because he now firmly believed in the age-old saying: elephants truly never forget.

The pain in my shoulder was excruciating as I got to my feet that sundown. It was the third sundown since the two leggers had patched me up; I could smell their presence on my skin when I first regained consciousness, and knew that they had tried to help me. I'd had plenty of experience with their methods, and had actually grown quite comfortable with the gentler ones among them. But this time the wound was deep and nauseating; it seemed to have a life of its own.

Though I dreaded to admit it, I sensed that this might be the beginning of the end. If it didn't get better soon, there might not be many nights left. I had a vision of my final hours, and this desolate, barren landscape was not in it. No, I wouldn't stop walking until I saw that vision unfolding in front of me.

I noticed several interesting things about the two-leggers who had come from the false beasts. I recognized their scents on the trail ahead, and realized that they were aware of me, but were keeping their distance. And they had left behind sweet grasses and vegetables that I would come upon and browse, left in the same manner as my food had been left in every place I had lived with the two-leggers. Lastly, I could feel a recognizable vibration deep in my ear, but its cause was not visible to my old, clouded eyes. The vibration, I realized, was from a false bird way, way up in the clouds. It had been there almost constantly for the last three days. Watching me, I now knew.

Chapter Fifteen

New York, 1974

In almost every life there is a moment where a choice is made that changes everything from that point on, thought Amanda many years later. The road not taken, the courage to speak up or remain silent in the face of a bully, the career chosen or abandoned, the lover married or spurned—the decision and its effects are only apparent with time. And there is no way to go back and change it. For better or worse, a life's course is set from that moment on.

Amanda experienced such a moment when she met a bearded, charismatic young man she felt within minutes would be the first great love of her life. She was in her junior year and in thrall with the city; she had blossomed into the beauty that had lain dormant in her all along. She was on the Dean's List and was stringing occasionally for Esquire Magazine, Cream and Rolling Stone, writing small pieces that she hoped would lead to bigger ones upon graduation.

He was auditing a popular lecture series when she met him; she later found he wasn't even enrolled at Columbia, but that almost made him more interesting. Ariel Levine was five years older than she, the first lover she'd had who was not within her class year. He was darkly handsome and of Jewish heritage, though he was far from a believer.

He was also the most evolved lover she had ever had, and he opened her up to ways of experiencing intimacy that were way beyond her years. They would take weekend trips upstate by train, making copious, aching love in the woods, in friends' houses, in communes, many times exploring the hallucinogens of the day—psilocybin, LSD, and mescaline (Amanda's favorite, because there were no downsides like nausea or dark, terrifying wormholes). The intense bonding during these "trips" made them so close it was almost scary.

His life's passion was one of hers as well: he was an animal lover of almost extreme proportions. His Australian shepherd was always at his side—Max would wait patiently wherever they went, without need of a leash—and Ariel's philosophy was like hers: he was a vegetarian, never wore animal hides like leather, and shunned all animal captivity. Where he differed from Amanda was that he was a member of an animal rights group that he had co-founded with a handful of like-minded friends. Based on radical groups that were just emerging in Europe, their passion bordered on the messianic. She soon became a member as well, picketing outside Fifth Avenue stores ("Your Mink Squealed in Agony as it Died"), picketing zoos ("You are Supporting a Maximum Security Prison Today"), then graduating to splashing red paint on Park Avenue matrons' furs and infiltrating audiences at fashion shows to spring up and splash fur-clad models on the catwalks.

In the coming years, their model would inspire groups like The Animal Liberation Front and eventually PETA, the gentler, commercial version of its predecessors. But in 1974, there was no model to learn from; it was all seat-of-the-pants trial and error. It linked the two lovers together in an intense, passionate commitment, and it wasn't until later that Amanda realized she was the follower, and he was the leader. It bordered on being cultish. She swore she would never cede her power like that again, but she had to learn her lesson the hard way.

The warehouse was located on a cul de sac overlooking a marsh in a grimy industrial area just outside Trenton, New Jersey. The five-member group had scouted it for a week, teams of two pulling twelve hour shifts until they knew the routines like clockwork. The "scientists," glorified technicians, really, arrived at nine and left at six each night, with a lone, unarmed guard left behind to oversee the research lab and its inhabitants: rats, monkeys, cats and dogs who were being used to test the side effects of products made by a multi-billion dollar cosmetics company.

Ariel explained to Amanda what that "testing" entailed; forcibly restraining the animals and then spraying solvents into their eyes, or forcing a perfume's ingredients down their throats in order to see what effect the chemicals might have. They would record the animals screeching, howling, twitching and convulsing. Then they would vivisect them before administering a fatal dose of strichnine in their IVs. Eventually they were cremated.

To Ariel, this was torture and murder of sentient, innocent creatures in the service of nothing but human vanity. Medical research was bad enough, but one could at least make the argument that those animals were dying in the service of finding cures for diseases. The cosmetics labs made his blood boil and brought tears to his eyes; he truly felt that all the humans involved along the line should be treated to the same prolongued, agonizing death.

The plan was for Amanda to distract the guard at the double glass front doors while the other members of the team waited at the rear service entrance, a corrugated steel roll-up door 200 feet and several walls away. The guard might be suspicious of a pretty young female with car trouble in the middle of an industrial park at two in the morning, but he'd at least make a call for her if he didn't open the door and let her in. In either case, it would give the rest of the team enough time to gain entry and start liberating the animals. In the monkeys' case, their cages would be stowed in one of two vans for a three-day drive to Louisiana, where Cajun Sammy, the group's high school-dropout and de facto enforcer, would release the monkeys in his old bayou haunts.

Amanda got Ariel to promise that, no matter what happened, there would be no violence. She was sometimes worried by his powerful emotions, but she was not mature enough yet to see clearly the hypnotic effect he had on her—as well as on the other members of the group.

Everything went according to plan at first, but rarely does any plan go off without a hitch, no matter how well rehearsed. The weather was ideal—a thick fog billowed off the marsh and covered the park in silence—and the guard, a short, overweight Slav in his fifties, fell for Amanda's act without hesitation. She was in the front office with him in seconds, where he dialed an all-night gas station, but they had no mechanic on duty. So, being a kind, simple-minded gentleman and flirt, he asked her to show him to her car; he was a bit of a mechanic himself, he claimed, maybe he could start it.

As she walked him out into the fog, knowing there was no car to show him, she pretended to be utterly lost and led him away from the rear of the building. Suddenly he turned around and shone his flashlight back at the facility, thinking he'd heard something. Low voices. And animal noises, he was sure of it. His flashlight bounced its beam back at them from the fog; he whispered for Amanda to stay put, he was going to investigate. Panicked, Amanda called out loudly enough to warn her friends.

"Please don't leave me here. I'm kind of scared."

The voices stopped, but the unmistakeable screech of a monkey reached them. The guard turned toward Amanda, who now started to back away, and it hit him what was happening.

"You are a part of this?" he exclaimed, and then he ran back toward the front office.

Ariel and Cajun Sammy cut him off at the door. He reached for his sidearm, then realized he was weaponless, and a cry escaped him.

"Please don't hurt me, I only work here! I have nothing to do with how—"

Sammy took him down in a headlock and pinned his face to the concrete. Ariel stepped close and spat, "Where have I heard that one before?" And, in a stagey German accent, "I vas only following orders!"

Amanda arrived and stared down in concern as Sammy tied the man's hands behind his back, then hauled him to his feet.

"You're gonna have to sit this one out, Pops," he said as he pushed the guard inside and sat him down roughly in a chair, then ripped the phone out of the wall and used the cord to fasten the visibly trembling Slav to the chair. His nose was bleeding and his forehead had a small abrasion where it had made contact with the concrete, but he otherwise appeared fine.

Perhaps it was a misplaced emotion, but, as Amanda accompanied Ariel and Sammy out the door to finish the liberation of the animals, she felt a wave of guilt about having manipulated and betrayed the sweet, poorly-paid guard. A steely radical would have had no such compunctions, she knew, and she realized then and there that she was not cut out for this life.

But in the next moment, it was too late to entertain such frivolous thoughts. A clogged left anterior descending artery in a frightened, mildly obese fifty-two-year old male with undiagnosed atherosclerosis suddenly occluded completely, and the guard leaned forward in agony and tried to cry for help, but all that came out was a groan through a clenched jaw. He was overwhelmed by a high-pitched whine in his ears that then stopped, replaced by a warm, soft sigh as his heart stopped sending blood to his brain. In seconds he was unconscious and without a pulse.

When the group had finished their work they left with a cursory check on him through the glass doors and assumed from his drooping head that he'd fallen asleep. It wasn't until two days later that one of their team, Jeffrey Southcott—his trust fund was their primary source of funding—walked into Ariel's East Village apartment holding a New York Post and a look of shock.

The New Jersey police and the FBI were on the trail of a radical group of animal activists for the murder of a security guard at a medical research facility in Trenton, NJ. Damek Radovan Zornow had been found dead after being bound and beaten while his murderers broke into the facility's laboratory and released or stole all the lab's animals. There was a $50,000 reward being offered for information leading to the arrest and conviction of four men and one woman seen leaving the scene in two Ford Econoline vans. A surveillance camera in the industrial park had captured the vans entering and then leaving; though the license plates had been obscured by the suspects, authorities were confident they would have them in custody in a matter of days.

To someone like Amanda, this news struck her so hard that she became light-headed and had to sit down, and then tears of panic and anguish flooded out of her. Her whole life, her entire future, was now in jeopardy because of the stupidest mistake she'd ever made.

Whatever he really felt, Ariel gave the impression that he was not worried; these clowns had no way of tracking them, he claimed, everyone should just go to ground. Find a place to stay until the heat was off. They got into this together, they would get out of it together. Cajun Sammy would stay put when he reached Louisiana, Jeffrey the heir would drive to his family's summer house in Maine, Peter the science major would take the train to San Francisco and crash with his brother, and Amanda and Ariel would stay with some sympathetic friends at their cabin in the Catskills. It would all blow over in a matter of weeks, he promised.

But Amanda knew it wouldn't blow over, and her opinion of Ariel and his schemes was changing fast. At the cabin, she began to see him clearly for the first time, and it shook her. When the story hit the nightly news on the local channels, she knew their time was short. The authorities claimed they had names now, which they would not release until the suspects were in custody. Ariel scoffed, but Amanda knew it was not a bluff. They were going to be hunted down, it was just a matter of time.

Her nights were long and filled with the most intense dreams of her life; the days were a succession of hours that crawled by as if the earth's gravity had tripled. She took long walks with Max in the high forest that bordered the cabin, trying to plan a way out of this nightmare. It was late October, yet she barely registered the stunning fall foliage.

It had occurred to her what to do right away, but she needed to build up the resolve to justify it and see it through. The next day she offered to go into town to buy groceries; she was getting cabin fever, she said. Ariel, who was descending into depression even as he denied it, grunted his approval.

She drove the four miles into town. At the lone gas station she looked around to make sure no one had followed her, then stepped into the phone booth. Through a friend, she knew of an attorney in New York City who had defended several radicals in notorious cases. When he came on the line she told him her story, and he agreed to meet her if she could get back to the city. He told her there was a way of surviving this, that she should act completely normal until she could get away from the cabin. Don't say goodbye or leave a note. Just get away.

That night she made love to Ariel with a tenderness she had not felt since their first nights together. When he realized she was crying as they lay there afterwards, he held her close, whispering that everything would turn out okay. At this, she sobbed even harder.

The next afternoon she took her daily walk through the forest, this time without Max, and kept going until she reached town. There she hitched a ride out of the mountains and, that night, slept in a park. The next morning she hitched a ride into the city.

The attorney was a character out of a Tolkien novel, she thought as they met in a midtown cafe. Just over five feet tall with wild silver hair and beard, he wore a cape and walked with a fancy cane. Meyer Goldman was unlike any man she'd ever met, but his obvious brilliance and frenetic energy somehow reassured her.

He was already in contact with the District Attorney's office, who had proposed a tentative deal: If everything she said turned out to be true, and if she could lead them to the ringleader, she would have a very good chance of avoiding prison. She would have to testify to everything that had happened, and then she would have to leave the country. In exchange for her testimony, all charges against her would be dropped, but she would be quietly, and permanently, deported.

After their meeting, Amanda walked the streets of Manhattan with an aching heart. Not only would she have to betray a lover, she would never again get to walk these pulsing, dirty, magnificent streets she so loved. Oh, how the decisions we make can turn us upside down, she thought bitterly.

She returned to their fourth-floor walkup in the Village and sat in the fading light until she worked up the courage to call him. She then confessed to a highly agitated Ariel that she had fled the cabin in depression, confusion and fear, and now that she was back in the city she regretted it terribly. She agreed that it had been a dangerous, risky, stupid move, and she wanted a second chance. Would he accept her back? Would he perhaps like to come back to the Village instead? No one was watching their apartment, everything seemed totally cool…?

The FBI agents who met with her in Meyer Goldman's office the next morning seemed sympathetic, or at least gave the appearance of it. The preliminary autopsy on the security guard verified what Amanda had told Goldman, that the man had not been beaten or treated badly; the likely cause of death was a stroke or a heart attack, but that would still result in charges of second degree murder.

Based on a map she drew, they laid out the best place to take Ariel into custody, where a minimum of force could be used and where there would be a minimal flight opportunity. She might very well be saving his life, they told her, since he would be unarmed and out in the open; in any other scenario, all bets would be off.

Amanda agreed to the plan, signed the D.A.'s offer, and was driven back to the Catskills in a small convoy. Three miles outside of town she was placed in a VW van driven by a female agent who looked like she'd just come from Woodstock. The agent dropped Amanda at the gas station and drove off.

Amanda called from the same payphone and was picked up by her hosts, a couple in their early thirties, an hour later. When they arrived, they seemed to be watching every car and every face in the vicinity. When she got into their creaky old Volvo, they were a lot less pleasant than they'd been before she left. They let her out when they got back to the cabin and walked inside without so much as a word. She realized they had only been feigning friendliness before; their true colors were now evident. She prayed that Ariel had not gone to the same place, that he was still on her side.

He was cool upon seeing her, but by dinner he was back to his old, confident self, and the four of them got stoned on hash and had an awkward meal together. Though her hosts' behavior toward her unnerved Amanda, it gave her a perfect excuse to ask Ariel to take a walk with her. She wanted to speak to him alone.

They started out from the cabin as the sun set, and Max bounded across the high meadow that led up to the forest. Amanda's heart was pounding so hard she almost called it off, but then she saw the first figure step from the trees and it was too late. Max began barking ferociously, and then more figures materialized from behind them and on both sides. As Ariel realized what was happening, he groaned and the air went out of him. Guns were drawn and there were shouts to get on the ground, and then Max was beside his master trying to protect him.

"Don't hurt the dog! Please don't hurt the dog!" Ariel shouted, and then a thick blanket was thrown over Max and two agents pinned him underneath it; Amanda had made them promise to take Max without resorting to violence.

Both she and Ariel were handcuffed and read their rights, and then cars were racing across the meadow toward them. Each was put into a separate car; the look Ariel gave her as the doors closed was, surprisingly, one of deep regret.

It didn't dawn on him until days later that she had given him up. He tried to reach her from prison several times while he was awaiting trial, but she couldn't bring herself to respond. Waiting in the bustling hallway outside the courtroom five months later, Amanda nearly passed out, stricken by guilt and remorse. She quietly announced to Meyer Goldman that she couldn't go through with it.

Goldman took her into a side chamber with one of the prosecutors, Greta von Helling, who Amanda had come to know when they'd rehearsed her testimony. After they'd taken seats at the conference table, Meyer spoke in a quiet but forceful tone.

"Amanda, this may be a very noble gesture, but if you back out now, you'll be destroying your life. Ms. Von Helling here will be forced to press charges against you and you'll go to prison for a minimum of five years— at the end of which you will be deported. Is that what you really want?"

Amanda sobbed. Ms. Von Helling reached over and held her hand.

"Miss Hathaway, I don't want to see you throw your life away for this guy. Mr. Levine orchestrated the whole thing, you were just an unwitting victim. He's going to prison even if you go back on our deal. Please, don't let him do this to you."

A few minutes later they walked her into the courtroom and she took the stand. Ariel sat with his public defender, staring balefully at Amanda, but she never looked him in the eye, even when asked to point him out. She left immediately after her testimony, and the next day was on an airplane bound for London.

CHAPTER SIXTEEN

Kenya and Beyond, 1974-1977

WHEN KAMAU RETURNED HOME from Nairobi that Christmas, he was in line to graduate with multiple offers in private veterinary medicine if he so desired, or a position in the Wildlife Service. Since he wanted to work with wild animals, as well as in the new government, there was no question which path he would choose, even if it meant less money.

He'd also fallen in love for the first time in his life, with a bright, quiet Kikuyu girl whom he had deftly maneuvered into being his study partner in third year biology. She was the most beautiful girl Kamau had ever laid eyes on—such is the way of limerence, but in Makena's case, she was the most sought-after girl in their class—and they were eventually engaged. This was hard for Makena's parents, who were more educated and westernized than Kamau's, but they eventually came around because their daughter was so obviously happy and in love, and because Kamau was so respectful, intelligent and kind that he was bound to have an excellent future.

Over a sumptuous dinner at Salisbury on Kamau's first night back from visiting his parent's village, Jean and Russell delicately broke the news that Ishi was missing. No one had seen him in over a year, and Jean and Russell were worried that he might have been killed; he was so friendly to humans that it might have been his downfall. His adopted herd had been spotted in Amboseli, but Ishi was not among them. This by itself was alarming, but worse, there were a half-dozen other white hunters in Kenya and Tanganyika who knew him by sight, and none of them had spotted him either.

Kamau was heartsick at this news; their bond was so strong that it rivaled his closest human relations. He had two weeks before he had to be back at university; he would take as much of that time as he could to find his dear friend—or at least find his remains.

Russell requisitioned one of Lord & Stanley's bush planes and a pilot to take Kamau—and Kagwe, as his tracker and protector—to scour herds within a 150-mile radius. Once they spotted one they would swoop in low, and if they identified a likely suspect, they would land somewhere nearby and hike back to the herd on foot. It would be a long and arduous process, but to a Kikuyu who had been raised on the rhythms of nature, who had spent days and nights sleeping with Ishi's herd, it was nothing. And he owed it to Ishi.

* * *

Just as Kamau had dreams of becoming part of his country's future, Gichinga Kimathi had his own dreams of climbing the ladder, but a slightly different version of it. He had landed in Nairobi after his poaching days in Voi town had become too difficult to juggle with his government job. Debt collecting had come easily to Gichinga—he was the most effective collector in the region, no doubt due to his persuasive ways— but he knew there was no future in intimidating deadbeats; he wanted something more. Much more.

In the Kenyatta regime, as in most post-colonial African countries, corruption was endemic. To play by the rules would lead to a career of slow, incremental promotions that would leave one at the mercy of corrupt, punitive bosses. Gichinga knew he was cut out to be one of those bosses; he saw his future in the upper halls of the government, even in the company of the Kenyattas. Someone had to end up in that small circle. Why not him?

To that end he came up with a coldly brilliant plan to shortcut years of toil in the bureaucracy. His success in Voi had led to a plum offer in the Nairobi Collections Department, and within months he was being invited to meetings and parties where he came into contact with higher-ups as well as other young men like him, cunning, ruthless, and willing to cut any corner.

Gichinga's immediate boss was wary of him. The rumor in the agency was that Gichinga had been so effective in Voi town because he had no scruples about hurting people, to the point that the only non-collections in his portfolio somehow ended up leaving the area. Quite an amazing record. But in the end his boss had no reason to fear Gichinga, because Gichinga had his sights set on much bigger game.

He had met the head of the Collections Department one weekend at a seminar and ingratiated himself with just the right amount of flattery and self-confidence. Mwangi Karanja and his pretty, much younger wife, Maina, appeared to be impressed, if a little dismayed, by his intense manner—his laugh was just as big and dramatic as his scowl—but they seemed to like him, as did Karanja's two teenaged children. Like many sociopaths, Gichinga was extremely adept at mimicking real emotions when he needed to, and now he employed that gift in the most important performance of his life.

Karanja was a holdover from the colonial era, and had been promoted to the top job when Kenya gained independence. He was trained in the civility and patience of the old regime, and was therefore not nearly as ambitious as the new members of the government, nor as circumspect as he might have been. Karanja was so impressed by Gichinga's leadership qualities that he set Gichinga up just down the hall from his office, and soon gave him the coveted job of supervising all field agents.

The Karanjas eventually started inviting him over for dinners on weekends, and then to their place in Mombasa, where they kept a thirty-foot sport-fisher that harked back to Karanja's youthful days as a fisherman. There they heard the tragic story of Gichinga the widower—how his wife and child had been killed in an auto accident in Eldama Ravine several years ago—and they were moved by his compassion and obvious pain.

Within months, Karanja asked him to be his successor when he reached retirement, some five years off. But more telling, Maina had started to show feelings for this virile, tempestuous man her age. On a few occasions, like when they passed each other in the sport-fisher's tight cabin belowdecks, they brushed against each other and electricity shot between them. Soon it led to passionate kissing, their hands running over each others' bodies, but each time Gichinga the actor whispered that they couldn't go through with this, they both loved Karanja too much.

A few weeks later Karanja disappeared on his way home from work and was never seen again. His car was found in a marsh several months later, but there were no clues as to what had happened. No known enemies, no signs of a struggle; no body, no blood, no note, and the case went nowhere.

Maina was beside herself with grief, and probably some guilt at her having secretly betrayed her husband with his employee. Karanja's two children were devastated, but as time passed and they had to return to their college lives, a new mourner appeared in the Karanja home. Gichinga was there for Maina in her hour of need, and after the appropriate amount of mourning, their lovemaking, freed at last, was so fierce it almost raised the dead.

In the end, Gichinga took over Mwangi Karanja's position as head of the Collections Dept. with little opposition, and he and Maina were married in a private ceremony at sea, after which the newlyweds sold the sport-fisher. It harbored too many memories.

* * *

When I look back on the time I traveled with Big Black and his bachelor clan, I can fool myself into thinking it wasn't such a difficult period. In my current state, I would gladly do it all over again. At the time, I didn't know how much I would miss it one day.

It took awhile before I finally gave up on the notion of finding Mother Blue's scent, and I adjusted to the habits and the pecking order of the herd as they trailed behind the angry rump of their demented leader. Each day took us further and further away from my old world into lands I never knew existed. I saw creatures I'd never seen before, and endless expanses of water and forests and mountains. Even the grasses and trees were new to me.

As free as it felt to roam new lands, there was a weight I always carried: I was a creature of habit, and my emotions were tied to the places where I'd been born and raised, which were never more than a few days' walk from each other. Now I was like a newborn, but without a guiding mother. I had to rely on my new friends for everything. Over time our bonds grew quite powerful, if not the equal of a mothers' love and guidance.

I was growing larger and stronger by the day, so the challenges from the other adolescent bulls were rare, and when they did happen—there was one bull named Boomer who hated me from the moment he laid eyes on me—I was always able to give as good as I got. Big Black encouraged these rivalries, but wouldn't allow any goring. It would have led to needless deaths, and he threatened to hunt down and kill any bull who crossed that line.

In the end, Big Black may have been crazy, but he had a lifetime of stories and was always fair in his rule. I didn't realize how much he'd mean to me until he was gone, and how much wisdom he'd brought to the clan. His passing, from an unseen sickness eating at his insides, was the moment I became a fully mature bull. From then on, I could survive on my own, though I hoped never to have to.

We were laying over at the greatest chasm of water any of us had ever seen. A wide river swept over a cliff and crashed to the rocks far below, sending up a deafening roar and a mist that danced with colors like after a rain. Big Black had planned on ending up at this place all along; this was where he had been born. Now we would watch over him as he lived out his final moments. He couldn't even eat the grasses and soft bark we had been bringing him to keep his stamina up.

We all said our remembrances as he lay there, his eyes fixed on some place only he could see. We stood guard as he breathed his last, then covered him with fresh branches and quietly filed away. No one spoke for the remainder of that day, because we all knew we would not stay together without Big Black to bind us.

The next morning Boomer charged me without warning. Little Stream sent up an alarm and I turned just in time. We fought for the entire day, but without Big Black's rules, Boomer was quite willing to use his tusks to try and wound me. This was a battle for the succession of the clan, I quickly realized, and though I could have turned and run at any time, something inside me would not relent. As the rest of the bulls watched, with no intention of interfering, we traded blows so savage we shuddered and sometimes fell.

By nightfall we were both so exhausted and sore it was decided that we should carry it over until the next morning, and both of us were separated by the herd to make sure nothing unfair occurred. I had hurt Boomer, I knew this from his breathing and a limp in his hind legs, but I didn't know how severely. Then, in the morning, I found out. He could hardly stand, and he announced with a pained, but sufficiently contrite tone, that he was quitting the fight. I had won. And like I had witnessed with my mother and She Storms so many seasons ago, the herd split up that morning, four bulls going with me, and three with him.

We said our goodbyes, knowing we'd probably cross paths at some point, and I led my little clan back the way we'd come. I wasn't prepared to be a leader at my young age, but I was as strong and intelligent as any of us, so it fell to me. I asked my mates to share in all the tasks of leadership; I did not need or want to be singled out, and they all readily agreed. If there were disagreements among us, or a lone voice was needed, I would take that role.

This had the unintended result of making us a tight-knit clan that traveled quickly and with no craziness. When we would come across other herds, I was acknowledged as the ranking bull, and if there were no older rogue bulls about, I had my choice of the most eligible cows in estrus. This was a new development that followed my having come of age, and females had started inviting me to mount them. It was exhilarating. In the coming years, I was proud to find that I had sired several calves. My seed would carry on for generations.

We made it back in time for the annual gathering of the herds, a rainy season event that brought clans from many horizons away. The strict, female-driven rules were relaxed for a time and bulls were welcomed back to their birth herds, reconnecting and trying to forge new "relationships" with their female cousins and friends.

My bachelor clan dissolved temporarily so we could each visit our old herds, spread out over a great plain below the snow-capped mountain we all knew as the center of the world. We agreed to meet up afterwards and continue our travels together. I would send out a message when it was time.

I walked among the countless herds, looking at faces and scenting for signs of Mother Blue and my adoptive aunties and friends. Hopefully they had re-assembled after the great fire, and I would see the delight in their eyes when they realized I was alive and had grown into adulthood.

A very desirable female ran up to me at one point and tried to excite me. Suddenly a massive bull came into view with liquid streaming down his face and shoved me aside. His unsheathed impregnator swung precariously between his legs, and the young female took off running again. She was not going to escape this bull's advances for long.

After I got back to my feet and pressed on, I heard a familiar voice rumble somewhere nearby and my heart skipped. I looked up and recognized a pair of drooping, tear-filled eyes and bellowed loudly. It was Sad Eyes, my old mate from the big cat episode! And then a big round head looked up from a nearby stream. Mother Blue! And several more of my old herd and some new arrivals as well. I ran up to them, and what was left of my old aunties and friends assembled around me and scented every inch of me, and I them. I was deliriously happy, and we stayed like that for some time until I asked—

"Where is everybody else? Crooked Mouth, Tiny Feet, Little Tail...?"

Mother Blue sighed painfully. "We never saw them again, dear Ishi. We were hoping to run into them here, but we fear they may have perished in the fire like we feared you had. Or been cast to the far lands with no way back to us."

I spent several days with my old herd, and the kindness Mother Blue and the others showed me made me realize I would have been able to stay with them for many more seasons if the fire had not separated us. It made my heart ache with sadness, but not regret. I had chosen to go with Big Black's clan, and I could never regret that. It was just how things turned out, and now that I was a grown bull, I didn't need the succor of females anymore. I could never go back.

My little bachelor herd, with the addition of two brothers and another bull who'd decided to join us after the gathering, made its way back along the route we'd traveled with Big Black two seasons ago. When we came upon the burned landscape where we'd first met—it was now covered with rich grasses and new growth on the blackened trees—I realized we were getting close to home. I was feeling slightly anxious about what to expect in my new role as leader of a clan in my old territory.

I remembered the second most important rule of life, but I should have paid more heed: When things are going well, embrace the days, because they never last for long. A dark wind is always waiting over the horizon, and it can come racing down the plains at any moment.

We were eating in a grove of trees amidst high brush, seemingly protected from view, when the echo of a boom stick shattered the silence. I wheeled and saw Little Stream wince, a puff of dust pluming from his head, and fall heavily. I recoiled, then shouted for the others to run. In the next instant another boom stick sounded, and one of our new males fell. I couldn't see where the two-leggers were located—we had not heard or scented them—but I had to choose an escape route immediately and hope it was away from them. The others stormed after me into the grove, and we didn't stop until we were gasping in a wooded hollow beneath a distant hill.

I felt overwhelming anguish. I had lost a dear friend, and I had let my clan down. Seeing my grief, my brothers drew close to me and assured me there was nothing any of us could have done. The cruelty of the two-leggers was a constant for all of us on the plains, and we had to accept it as part of life. But my heart ached; I loved Little Stream and his sweet ways, and I would mourn him for many seasons. He was also the last connection to my birth clan, and, except for my memory, I now had none.

* * *

Colin Woodleigh, a bearded, pipe-smoking 58-year old white hunter, watched the young bulls through his binoculars as they grieved over two fallen comrades. The bachelor herd's leader, who was young for the role, seemed to be taking the deaths harder than the other four. If these young bulls survived, he thought, all of them would be worthy of trophies in a few years, but only the leader had a pair of tusks worth taking now.

But that was not why the old white hunter watched. He had walked in from his Land Rover early that morning with his spotter to set up a blind for their client, who wanted to bag a leopard, and they'd inadvertently come across this sad scene. Something was eating at Woodleigh's memory: This young bull was somehow familiar to him. He had perfect recall of every elephant in Amboseli, but this one was from one of the nearby parks, he was pretty sure of it. Tsavo, he thought. Something about the tear in his left ear; there are always identifiers from life's travails in an elephant's ears.

Something jogged his memory and he glassed the bull's forehead carefully. Sure enough, there it was: The scar above his trunk, faint but visible to a trained eye. It was his old friends Russell and Jean Hathaway's first orphan calf, thought to have perished two or three years ago. Well, he thought, this will make for a nice surprise.

Russell got there that evening and found Ishi still at the scene of his friends' deaths, keeping the hyenas and vultures at bay, rushing them whenever they made a move. Ishi was so preoccupied he hadn't heard or scented the Land Rover. Russell walked out into the open and let Ishi see him, then called to him. It had been almost three years, and he didn't know for certain if Ishi would recognize him. The other bulls gathered around their leader and seemed to be deciding whether to charge.

Ishi rumbled something to them and then walked out to his old friend. Russell smiled with delight, even as he knew Ishi was in a somber mood. As he stroked Ishi's head and whispered comfortingly, as Ishi caressed his entire body with his trunk, Russell debated what had to be done. Ishi's two mates had been shot for their tusks, and it was apparently just dumb luck that Ishi had been spared. With poaching having reached epidemic proportions in the last few years, he knew Ishi wouldn't last long here.

After spending several minutes with his old friend, Russell said his goodbye and climbed back into his Land Rover. He realized that what he had to do would upset several people who were extremely close to him if they ever found out, so he swore Colin to secrecy: Ishi had not been seen in three years, was presumed dead, and it would stay that way.

CHAPTER SEVENTEEN

England and Beyond, 1977-1982

BELOWDECKS, THE ENGINE hummed and throbbed, changing pitch as the waves lifted and dropped the old freighter in the heavy seas. The entire length of the steel hull groaned.

To an elephant enclosed in a barred cage in the bowels of the stern, this was other-worldly in the extreme. Nothing like this had ever occurred to Ishi in his wildest imaginings. It was so nightmarish that he could do nothing but fix his gaze on a small porthole and try his mightiest to keep his balance as the ship rolled. He had already been slammed into the cage wall several times, and it left him bleeding.

The journey had begun under light cloud cover, and the sea had been relatively calm for the first few hours. Then darkness fell and the storm hit with an announcement of thunder and lightning. The elephant was used to being out in weather, but only on solid ground. He trumpeted in desperation, but his keeper, the two-legger who had accompanied him on the long overland journey in a large false beast, was nowhere to be found.

The most confusing thing of all was how he had come to be here in the first place. He had been wallowing in the mud beside a river with his fellow bachelors when he'd smelled and then recognized his old two-legger "father," who he'd seen just days before, and he had sauntered over to exchange greetings. The two-legger had a group of friends waiting in the distance in their false beasts. There was something amiss in his friend's eyes and tone, Ishi could sense it. Suddenly he felt a sharp sting in his hide. He turned to see what it had been, but it was out of sight in his hind quarters. He noticed that his two-legger friend was now standing at a distance from him, and there was clearly something different in his behavior.

Then a warmth and a darkness swept over him and he felt so dizzy he had to sink to his knees. Moments later he rolled onto his side, and the last thing he remembered was his friend near his head, stroking his face in that wonderful way that had always given him such a good feeling. His friend was whispering words that Ishi could not understand, but they were more for the two-legger's benefit anyway.

"I'm terribly sorry, old friend…but we don't really have a choice." Then he signaled his waiting companions to bring their false beasts.

"You'll be well-treated, I promise. And I'll come visit you…"

Ishi's eyes rolled back in his head and he felt himself falling down an impenetrably dark tunnel, but as he put his legs out to break the fall, there was nothing there.

* * *

Ishi had no concept of how long this ocean journey would last. Could it be for the rest of his life, he wondered? If so, if the separation from his world was this painful already, he would have to consider starving himself and ending it. The two-legger who had driven him across the jungles of central Africa to the coast and who now visited him twice a day to leave food, bathe him and clean out his cage, was not a very friendly sort. A light-skinned two-legger who used a nasty long stick to get his way, when softly spoken words would have been enough.

One night Ishi had a transcendent experience that nothing could have prepared him for. He heard, over the engine's thrumming, a long, high-pitched call that somehow communicated a lifetime of information to him. It was not in his language, and yet it was. He quickly realized there was another creature passing in the water somewhere. Then a second and a third creature responded, answering the first call.

He moved as close as he could to the open porthole, but his view was limited to a small slice of the horizon. He looked out anyway, hoping to catch a glimpse of one of them. Then he saw it, and it rocked him. One of them surfaced for a moment, sending up a hissing plume in the moonlight. Then it re-entered the water silently and disappeared. The singing began again, and the elephant was transfixed. He blurted something in his own tongue, but he knew it couldn't reach past the walls of his prison. As he'd surmised, there was no response.

These creatures were as big as he was, he realized. Bigger, even. But their world was in this immense water, where they must rule as magnificently as his own kind did on land. This night gave him hope again, that there were friends out there who he might one day meet. The thought of this kept him alive, kept him going, and the ocean journey now became bearable.

The ship docked at the port of Liverpool in a dark, evening drizzle, and eventually a giant crane lifted the elephant's cage up and out of the hold, whereupon he got a stomach-dropping view of the Mersey River and the teeming docks below. The harsh lights, smells and cacophony of the industrialized world assaulted his senses. His cage was lowered onto a semi's trailer and battened down by loud and ill-mannered two-leggers who reminded him of some tree-dweller clans back home. Then the truck lurched forward.

Three hours later, the truck backed up to a loading platform and Ishi was greeted by his new masters, who showed him more affection in the first few minutes than he'd received in the last several weeks. His cage door was lifted and he was directed, through soothing voices and gentle prodding, down the ramp and into the cavernous door of an old brick outbuilding. Once inside, the door was closed behind him and a door across the way rolled open.

He stood there for a moment, trying to regain his bearings; having been trapped in a 12' by 12' cage for so long, a bit of room was a revelation. As he took in his surroundings, he picked up the scent of other elephants on the dirt floor, but they were nowhere to be seen. A water trough and piles of vegetables awaited him, but he wasn't ready to eat just yet. He ventured out the door and looked around in the misty rain. The setup reminded him of his first years with his two-legger family; an expanse of ground with some barren trees and a watering hole. A steep, fifteen-foot concrete drop-off beyond it prevented escape. Past this "moat" it was dark, but he could sense unseen animals watching him.

He'd have to wait until morning to know for sure, but if this was going to be his new home, it was going to be a cold one.

* * *

One hundred-thirty miles to the south, twenty-two-year old Terence Hathaway sat backstage with his bandmates after opening for the X-Ray Spex at a packed, pulsating dance hall in Birmingham. He had become the bassist and backup singer in The Zeros, a punk band started by one of his friends. A year before, upon realizing that this new movement was a perfect fit for outliers—and it didn't require more than rudimentary musical skills—he taught himself to play bass guitar and adopted the stripped-down look: short, spikey hair, tight jeans and tees under a leather jacket, and a sardonic smile. He wasn't as angry or socially disruptive as the band's core members, but externally he was a perfect fit. His life was looking up after years of false starts, and this was the end of one of the best days of his life: a small independent record label had just signed them. It was only for 500 pounds, but it seemed like a million.

His lover of late was Christopher Leitch, a successful thirty-four-year old magazine photographer who seemed to genuinely like, and get, Terence. But Terence's deepest longings were never quite satisfied by love or friendship; there was a cavernous hole in him that no amounts of alcohol, marijuana or LSD could fill. As with so many of his generation, it was a combination of influences: the unintentional mistakes of his parents, the cruelty of his peers in his teens; the natural inclinations of a unique personality; and the genetic proclivity for addictive substances. Since heroin was in vogue again, freed from its 1950s stigma by artists from The Velvet Underground to the Rolling Stones, it hadn't taken long for Terence to get up the nerve to try it. His first high had gobsmacked him like nothing he'd ever known, filling his gnawing hole and then some. Terence welcomed it like a long-lost friend.

But it was no friend; it always disappeared, returning him to the world he was trying to escape. That night at the after-concert party, Terence, feeling impervious—manic would perhaps be a more accurate word—ended up overdosing. Christopher and two bandmates rushed him to the local hospital, where, after an hour of panicked waiting, Terence was finally revived.

If it was a wake-up call, it didn't last long. The warnings from the doctors, then from his mates, grew old after a few weeks and he was back secretly using, thinking he knew how to handle it now. It was, tragically but predictably, just a matter of time.

His sister had shown up in his life in the last few months after returning from America, and when she realized what he was doing, became even more alarmed than his friends. The next thing he knew, his mum was there and he was taken to a rehab facility outside of London and enrolled in methadone therapy. Jean rented a cottage down the road and visited him every day, attended therapy sessions with him, and alternately pleaded and cajoled that he had to stop. But a desperate, loving mother is no match for a drug like heroin in a son with an addictive gene. Upon his release from the clinic, after he had seen Jean off at the airport, he bought a dime bag from a street connection on his way back to his flat. Avoiding his roommates, he locked his door, crawled up on his bed, and shot the moon. Sadly, there was no white light waiting to greet him at the end of a dark corridor, no last memories or dreams to grace his final seconds. Just complete darkness as his heart suddenly stopped pumping blood to his brain. As if a plug had been yanked from a socket.

Amanda arrived the next morning to take him to their usual Sunday breakfast, and when she got no answer—his flat-mates were out—talked the building manager into letting her into his bedroom. That's where they found him, the syringe still in his arm, a faint smile on his face. Amanda fell to her knees beside the bed, then started slapping Terence's face and pounding on his chest. The manager bolted back down the stairs to call an ambulance, but there was no doctor or hospital that could bring Terence back.

The news reported that there had been a several fatal ODs that weekend due to a batch of virtually uncut brown heroin. Terence had, once and for all, drawn the short straw.

The telephone call to her mother, who had arrived back at Salisbury the next day, was the hardest Amanda would ever have to make. By then her emotions had run the gamut from hysteria to anger to hollowed-out, and her first words sounded like they were coming from a stranger's mouth.

"I'm sorry, who is this?" Jean asked after Amanda couldn't go on. "Amanda, is that you?"

"Mum… I'm so sorry, I have…the worst news imaginable."

"What is it?" Jean was able to ask, but she already knew what her daughter was going to tell her.

"It's Terence, isn't it? What's he done?"

Amanda was crying again, and no further words were needed. Jean shrieked and sobbed until Russell came running from the orphanage yard.

"What is it? What is it?" Russell demanded, but he knew from his wife's desolation what had happened and blindly stumbled from the house, fell to his knees, and wept for the first time in years.

The grief drove Jean into a temporary madness that neither her husband nor daughter could reach. The guilt she felt for having failed her son, the sheer agony of a mother losing a child, broke her. She met the coffin, and Amanda, at Nairobi airport with Russell and Kamau. After they'd buried him on the hill above Salisbury, she threw herself into caring for her second family, her orphans.

Though she shared her bed with her husband, Russell knew he'd lost her. There were other reasons for why they eventually divorced, but they both knew that losing Terence was the fatal blow.

* * *

Under the agreement her attorney had made with the U.S. Justice Dept., Amanda's deportation was kept a secret, even from the British government, and she never spoke of it again. After numbly partying for several weeks when she returned from burying her brother, she finally got the wherewithal to go looking for work. After what she'd just been through, she didn't really care if she was rejected, and that attitude— given the time and place—worked wonders. She was able to parlay her jobs with Esquire and Rolling Stone into part-time work at the Daily Mail, whose editors were looking for young journalists who could give them access to The Scene, and she was on her way.

She soon made a name for herself interviewing the stars of rock, film and television, and after a year on the entertainment beat wrote a serious spec story, much like the muckraking pieces she had written in boarding school, and left it on the desk of the front-page editor after his secretary had gone home for the night. He was duly impressed and called her in for an interview. After five minutes of listening to her intelligence and passion, he gave her a desk—over the objections of the older, male staff writers who didn't take keenly to a pretty redheaded "bird" joining their club—and eventually transitioned to a full-time job as an investigative journalist.

If only her taste in men had been as successful she would have had a good shot at happiness. But she always picked strong, virile men—versions of her father—who subsumed her, and though there was always intense passion, her trait of allowing herself to be overshadowed, of never truly confronting them with her feelings, led to the rotting away of the relationships' foundations, and, inevitably, to their collapse.

Her choice of husband seemed propitious at first. At 32, Geoffrey Walling wasn't the handsome alpha male she was usually attracted to; he was a pale, soft-spoken commercial director from London whose intelligence was his charisma. They got married when Amanda turned twenty-eight and she became a mother of twin daughters at thirty. This new role fulfilled her need to create a safe, loving environment she could control, at least for a few years. Unlike the loves she had known or the vagaries of her work, being the head of her own little clan gave her the best feeling she'd ever had.

Regrettably, Geoffrey turned out to be a magnet for other women as well. After spending a weekend with him while he was shooting his first feature in Aberdeen, Scotland, Amanda sensed something in his and his leading lady's interactions that, even though it had been subtle, set off alarms. She was a journalist, after all, and had developed a keen sense of interpreting peoples' behavior. When a production assistant drove her to the train station to return to London, she sat in her compartment for a moment, then bolted off the train just as the doors were about to close and took a taxi back to the hotel. She had kept her room key, and when she unlocked the door she found her husband in bed with the actress.

Too numb for tears, or anger, or even words, Amanda walked back out the door and headed for the station. She silently wept all the way to London.

As much as Geoffrey professed to rue his mistake, as much as he regretted losing Amanda, she knew she'd made the right decision to end the marriage rather than endure humiliation and betrayal again. Geoffrey eventually became a good friend, a respected film director (with a reputation for bedding beautiful women), and a devoted father to his daughters.

At least Amanda would always have her brood. And her work.

* * *

In his way, Russell grieved for his son as deeply as Jean, but as months of anguish settled over Salisbury, and the predictable recriminations of guilt and blame reared their heads, his grief became tinged with resentment. In an attempt to escape the cloud, he took a job with an old client who was flying to Masai Mara game reserve. Russell neglected to mention it would be a hunting safari.

He knew it could come back to haunt him, but he went ahead with it anyway, and later it occurred to him that he'd been unconsciously trying to end his marriage. The client, a wealthy Viscount, had an entourage of drunken, cocaine-addled friends (and their wives) who were first-time hunters. Russell enforced the rules of gun safety with a firm hand, but when you're in the wild with neophytes, loaded rifles and dangerous game, bad things can happen.

One of the friends ended up shooting a black rhino at close range—before Russell was in position to give the go-ahead—but didn't drop it. When it wheeled and charged, Russell had no clean shot without killing the client, so he ran out in front of the enraged beast to distract it. The ploy worked all too well.

As Russell tried to sprint away, the rhino caught his belt with its tusk and sent him flying. Russell slammed to the ground and rolled into a protective ball, knowing what was coming. The rhino lowered its head and drove into him. The tusk glanced off Russell's shoulder, mercifully, but then entered his cheek below his left eye. The rhino would have killed him with the next thrust, but Kagwe had grabbed the client's rifle and fired a bullet into the animal's heart from ten feet away, dropping it instantly.

Russell was rushed to Nairobi by air, but emergency surgery could only salvage the facial wound, not his eye. He would wear an eyepatch for the rest of his life, and when the scar faded with time, people remarked that he looked like a dashing old swashbuckler from a Hollywood movie.

Jean stayed at his bedside in the hospital as he recovered, but Russell knew he had betrayed her trust for the last time. When he came home, she had moved to the guest cottage, and when he was well enough, she informed him she was staying at Salisbury with her orphans—and would he please move out. It was over.

* * *

Kamau's years after veterinary school were a series of doors opening, one after the other, until he had risen to the top echelons of the Ministry of Wildlife. He had developed a dry, ironic wit that pilloried the unsuspecting, like older government bureaucrats, with only his friends in on the joke. He became infamous among the other young Kenyans making their way up the government ladder.

He and Makena and soon their children were invited to everyone's parties on the weekends. By thirty-two, he was working across the hall from the minister himself, but since he didn't have the instincts of a certain psychopath, he was happy to serve in whatever capacity he could, because his first love was the animals. He spent half his time in the field cultivating relationships with tribal villages, townships, and every hunter, rancher and farmer in service of the wildlife he was trying to protect. The other half of the job was trying to mitigate the damage the Kenyatta regime was doing to the animals. The government gave lip service to being anti-poaching but was secretly making a fortune selling ivory on the black market.

Kamau's deep love for elephants had only grown with age; he sought them out whenever he was in the field, always keeping an eye out for Ishi. Kamau could never accept the fact that Ishi was dead, and he would keep looking for him until they were somehow reunited, either here or in the next world.

CHAPTER EIGHTEEN

England and Kenya, 1983-1985

HOW LONG I HAVE BEEN in this place is hard to fathom, since the days are always the same; the same sky, the same food, the same walking in endless circles until sleep takes me. I feel that my time here, if added up, has been close to the sum of all my life before, but I cannot be certain. I have no desire to go on like this, but when I stop eating, the keepers force me into a tunnel where no one can see what happens. Then they place a hose down my throat and pour liquids into me, and after a few days of this torture I relent and begin eating their food again. To resist is futile, so I go on.

My neighbors are no help, since most of them are even more despondent than I am. Their stares are distant, as if their true lives stopped the moment they were taken from their worlds. Strangely, there is a small contingent of them who argue that this existence is better than the one we were taken from, because there are no predators, no floods or fires, no starvation. But they are from the weaker breeds and were always sleepwalking through their lives anyway. Those of us with strength and intelligence are the most affected, reduced to standing in little enclosures that are supposed to remind us of our homes, while two-leggers file past and stare in at us.

It was not always like this. When I first arrived here there were already two sisters in my enclosure. Though they were fully grown, they were only half my size and their ears and tusks were tiny. The stories they told of their lives before this place were horrifying. The two-leggers in their world would chain them and force them to haul trees through jungles and rivers until they collapsed. They were treated like the two-leggers' domestic beasts I would occasionally come across back in my world—but these were elephants!

In the little time I had with them, their gentle ways made me respect them as much as any elephants I had known. Then one day they were led out the door and I never saw them again. Along with all the friends I have known, I visit them every night in my sleep.

My keepers are a curious mix of two-leggers—most are kind, like my friends who raised me—and then there is a nasty, eye-shifting male who waits until no one is watching and punishes me for whatever transgression he feels I was guilty of that day. I have tried to please him, but nothing I do seems to soften his heart. And to retaliate would be awful, I know that for certain. For I have witnessed his rage on another friend.

After the wonderful sisters were taken from me, I was alone for a time, walking circles under the same cold sky as, in my head, I visited better times in my life. Then one day the door opened again and a female who looked like she could have been from my clan was led in. I was thrilled until I saw the look in her eyes. Wherever she had been had scarred her, inside and out. I waited and surreptitiously watched her for days; she was not ready to speak or do any more than silently follow the keepers' orders. She seemed to know their language already, so she must have spent time in their world.

Finally she spoke to me, late one night as we stood listening to our neighbors sleep. Her voice was frail, as if she had used it up. Her name was Tatiana, a two-legger name that she had been given many seasons ago after she was taken from her birthplace to another land across the great water. There she had been put aboard a long, snake-like false beast that carried her across mountains and rivers. Eventually she reached a clan of females much like her, all confined in barred enclosures in another snake-like beast. These females had been worn down like stones in a river, Tatiana saw, and, with a sick feeling, she realized that this would be her fate as well.

She watched as the other females filed into a cavernous enclosure and went to work. She was quickly taught what the two-leggers wanted, and if she didn't step fast enough she was punished with shouts, prods or painful blows. All, she soon discovered, in the service of pleasing crowds of two-leggers who would cheer and clap at them in the giant enclosure. The routines were not difficult, and most of the two-leggers who performed amongst them, riding on their backs and hanging from their trunks, were kind, but the trainers were brutal. They quickly got Tatiana to do what they wanted, and she was left alone.

They would travel every few days in the false snake until they reached a new two-legger nest, where they would perform the same tricks again and *again. This life went on for many seasons, and Tatiana developed deep bonds with her sisters as she was worn down like a stone in a river.*

Then one day everything changed. They had noticed that their keepers were fewer and fewer, their meals were down to half their usual allotment, and animals started to disappear. Soon their trainers had taken over the duties of the kinder two-leggers, who were now all gone. They heard other animals in their cages complaining bitterly as their giant snake idled in a forest in the freezing cold...and then it happened.

One of the trainers was cleaning out a big cat's cage when there was a deep roar, a scream, and the other two-leggers came running. Tatiana heard a boom stick echo several times, and soon she and the sisters saw their most hated trainer being carried past them, blood seeping from grievous wounds. The elephants knew he would not live out the day, and then they realized this was going to be the end of their lives here as well. The only question was whether it would lead to a better one...or an even worse one.

At this point Tatiana was overcome with emotion, and I stood by her as she wept. No more memories were shared that night, but I was overcome by a strange, powerful feeling for her. It was the first time in my life I felt like that for a female. And, sadly, the last.

* * *

Through all the travails of the last years, Jean never considered her life tragic. Even having lost Terence—the most overwhelming grief she had ever experienced—she felt blessed to be alive and lucky to have found such a powerful calling with her orphanage. She could fall asleep at night with her heart heavy but content in the knowledge that everything she could do had been done, so there was no reason to be maudlin. She knew this attitude was British, but more, it was her generation's. They had survived the Great Depression and a world-altering war without a second thought of their role in it all; they were fighters, they would stand up for what they believed was right, and whatever God decreed would be the outcome (though He'd certainly hear about it from them). It made their lives fairly simple to understand in a dark, complicated world.

When she first heard the news from her doctors in December 1983, she kept it to herself. Kamau and Makena, who would visit Salisbury on most weekends, couldn't help but notice: she was losing weight and had begun wearing a knit cap to hide her thinning hair. What had once been a honey-colored mane had gradually turned silvery white over the years—she never colored it—and was now coming out in wispy clumps. So one morning she handed a pair of scissors to Makena and asked her to cut it all off.

Russell was living in London, where he had gone to figure out what he was going to do with the rest of his life—he certainly couldn't guide safaris any longer—so he wasn't aware of a problem. And Amanda hadn't been to Africa since Terence was laid to rest, so she didn't see the ravages of her mother's radiation and chemotherapy. Jean swore Kamau and Makena to secrecy: she didn't want to be a burden on anyone.

Six months into her battle, Jean had grown so weary of the treatments, which brought her nothing but nausea, overwhelming fatigue and painfully aching bones, that when she received a likely prognosis of less than a year, she stopped all western medicine and decided to try alternative therapies. When she asked Kamau and Makena to put her in touch with a well-known healer, Kamau called Amanda and implored, without revealing the secret Jean had sworn him to, that she come home.

When Amanda saw her mother's condition she tried to hide her shock, but that didn't last through dinner. When her mother calmly told her what she was facing, Amanda was devastated. She felt even worse because she hadn't visited more, and now she was going to lose her.

"She's fifty-eight!" Amanda exclaimed as she and Kamau walked in the hills after dinner. "How do you get brain cancer when you're young and vital like mummy?"

"We have no answers," Kamau responded. "We have been wracking our brains since we found out. We are glad to have you here to share it with us, at least…"

"Did you call my dad?"

"Just after I called you. He said he will be here in a few days."

That night as Amanda lay beside her mother in her darkened bedroom, they came to a painful realization. There was no reason other than irrational emotions for Amanda to take a leave of absence, uproot her children and move to Africa when it could be six months, or it could be years.

"You have a life to live in England," mused Jean. "A family to take care of. A career. I can't have you stand around watching me disintegrate. It wouldn't be good for you—or me."

If Amanda had expected to be the one counseling a diminished mother, she was pleasantly surprised that Jean was still so strong.

"We'll talk every night," Amanda declared, stroking her mother's hands. Jean smiled ruefully.

"You'll get bored hearing the same thing every night."

"Stop it."

Jean closed her eyes, sighed.

"When things start to get worse, I'll let you know."

"Promise? No more martyr routine."

Jean nodded. "I promise."

"I'll be on the first plane home."

Then the most unexpected thing happened. Russell sublet his London apartment and moved back to Salisbury with no expectations of anything except to spend whatever time his ex-wife had left taking care of her. This in spite of her having thrown him out several years before. It floored everyone; as unapologetically male as Russell had always been, like having never changed a diaper, this was new behavior at age 58, and she fell for him all over again. Russell became Jean's primary caregiver, driving her to appointments in Nairobi, cleaning up after the unavoidable accidents, bathing and dressing her and trying not to let her spirits sink too low.

One night near the end, they had a conversation that stunned Jean to her core. Russell spoke of the many nights he had spent under the stars contemplating Man's place in the universe, of our lonely time on earth, so eloquently that she realized she didn't even know who he was, or who he had become, anymore. They'd slept through much of their relationship, and she desperately wanted more time to know this surprisingly unpredictable man again.

Then he took her hand—the hospice care nurse had removed the IV lines to make Jean more comfortable—and whispered, "I have a confession..."

She looked at him through her haze and smiled weakly. "You have a girlfriend."

He was unprepared for humor at this point. He smiled wryly.

"Several. All younger and prettier than the next."

In fact, Russell had transitioned to a new realm since moving back to London. The glances he would have expected from females in his prime had vanished. Having observed animals in the wild for years, he realized he was no longer a desired member of the gene pool. As breathtaking as this was at first, it was a passage he eventually embraced.

"Seriously. I want you to hear me."

She nodded. He went on.

"Ishi is alive."

Her eyes widened, her lungs sucked in a painful breath. "I found him in Amboseli twenty-odd years ago...and sent him somewhere he'd be safe."

She lay there, speechless. Russell could tell that she was relieved, on one hand—Ishi was closer to her than any animal she'd ever raised—even as she obviously felt betrayed.

"Where...did you send him?"

"Sheffield Zoo. They have a pretty decent elephant display, and they take good care of him." He trailed off, knowing how militantly Jean felt about zoos. "I wanted to tell you a thousand times...but I knew you'd be against it. I just couldn't let him be killed for his ivory."

He watched as a myriad of emotions crossed her face. With an exhalation of breath she finally whispered. "I forgive you."

Then, with tears welling in her eyes: "For everything."

When Amanda arrived the next day from London, there was no mention of Russell's betrayal; Jean knew she was close to death, and there was no reason to poison her daughter's feelings towards her father. She saw the wisdom of the choice he had made, even if she didn't agree with it.

Three nights later, as she looked up at the remaining loves of her life gathered around her bed—her ex-husband, her daughter, and her adopted son—she slipped into a deep, morphine-induced sleep that there would be no waking from.

Even though they'd gotten used to the idea of her leaving them, none of them could stop crying for days. And across an ocean five thousand-miles to the north, Ishi felt a wave of sadness wash over him inexplicably. He looked around to see what was wrong.

Nothing seemed amiss, but something was gone, he could feel it in his bones.

Chapter Nineteen

Zambia and Tanzania, Present Day

JEREMY WESTBROOK WANTED Trevor Blackmon as far from their elephant as possible, but he needed him to oversee the Zambian parks' end of things until they crossed into Tanzania in two days. When Westbrook confronted him with the mushroomed bullet sealed inside a plastic baggie, Blackmon had unexpectedly come clean.

"I assume you have an explanation for this," Westbrook said as he held the baggie up.

Blackmon was about to lie—but then caught himself.

"Aye. It was me," he admitted quietly. "I fired from the heli to get him to move. Without a clean target. A moment of madness, mate."

Westbrook stared at him, his worst suspicions confirmed.

"I knew it was wrong the moment I did it," Blackmon went on. "I can't take it back, but I desperately want to make amends."

"How do you intend to do that?" Westbrook asked. "You know the rules as well as anyone—your job is to *protect* wildlife, not kill it."

"I made a realization afterwards. It may sound crazy, but I'm a changed man, sir. On my honor."

Westbrook looked out at the moonlit clouds gathered over the border.

"Well, you told the truth like a changed man. I give you credit for that."

"Thank you, sir." Blackmon followed his gaze toward the clouds. "I expect I won't be seeing you people after you cross over in a couple of days...so I'd like to make a request. Is it possible that you could see clear to not mentioning this incident to anyone else?"

Westbrook knew that reporting him would end his career with the national parks. How he'd gotten the job in the first place was beyond him; Rebecca had learned that Blackmon had been a soldier for the Rho-

157

desian government, an apartheid state until it became Zimbabwe, so he doubtless had blood on his hands. He'd somehow disappeared into Zambia and joined the national parks service, hiding in plain sight.

"I'll have to think about it. Give me until tomorrow."

Blackmon took it like a man, held out his hand, and they shook.

There was no way this bastard should be anywhere near wild animals, thought Westbrook. He would file the report once they were in Tanzania; he figured Blackmon would catch on somewhere as a tour operator, or perhaps as a security consultant for the visiting Chinese ivory buyers. They deserved each other.

Watching the day's footage in his trailer that night, Westbrook could see the pain the old elephant carried from the shoulder wound—it had obviously not healed properly and was festering with bacteria—so he started a powerful course of antibiotics in the elephant's feed. It would hopefully knock back the infection and the accompanying pain without fatiguing him too severely.

He was such a noble creature, with such a titanic will, that by the end of the first week—even faster than Brandeis had predicted—the show was a hit. The old bull was imbued with great pathos by the narration of Morgan Freeman and a haunting, emotional score. Filling the rest of each hour was a simple task; footage of Ishi's early life at Salisbury and of his later years in Sheffield Zoo were interspersed with interviews of animal experts and stock footage of elephant life, which was inexpensive and dramatic. But mostly, the suspense of whether he would make it to see his old friends and his birthplace before he ran out of life was simply too much for most people to resist.

The border crossing was orchestrated so that there would be as little human interaction as possible. The two countries had their representatives standing by, Zambia's Trevor Blackmon handing off the duties to Tanzania's bespectacled parks warden, Abasi Thuku, and then night fell and the elephant disappeared into the first of three national parks that would give him safe passage home—from cities and cars, anyway.

CHAPTER TWENTY

England, Kenya and Beyond, 1986-1998

KAMAU HAD FINALLY HAD his fill of the Wildlife Ministry, where he worked with corrupt, uncaring bureaucrats under the new president, Daniel Arap Moi, who was even more ruthless and despotic than the Kenyattas. Since Arap Moi was not a Kikuyu, the positions at the top of the ministries were all being filled by his tribal friends, and Kamau soon realized his career was going to be stopped in its tracks. And with it the fate of the wildlife he had fought so hard to protect.

So when Russell and Amanda had sat down with him the day after Jean's funeral and made him an offer, it was the answer to all his prayers. They would be staying in England, they told him, and wondered if he and Makena would like to take over the orphanage.

"This may surprise you," added Russell quietly, "but when we first met you, Jean said she thought you'd run the orphanage one day. Was she right?"

Kamau was speechless; in fact he was so overwhelmed that tears sprang from his eyes. This brought Amanda to tears as well, and she embraced her African brother as he wept.

"I am so happy to say yes to you both," Kamau managed to get out. "You are my true family, maybe even equal to my own."

For Kamau, it had been a return to his second home, where he could carry on his work as well as the work of his beloved second mother. The pay from donations was modest, and he and Makena didn't have the social life of a rising government official, but Salisbury offered its own rewards. Instead of a cramped apartment in a noisy, polluted city, they woke up to the serenity of a sprawling house overlooking a landscape that rivaled any in the world. And the orphaned animals filled their days and their hearts. If Kamau regretted not becoming the important minister he had once set out to be, he soon made peace with it, and realized this was where he belonged for the next period of his life. This, he realized, was how one's destiny worked out sometimes.

Russell returned to England and reconnected with his old world for the first time in forty years. He had been reluctant to do so while there was still a chance at making it work with Jean, but now the future was disconcertingly wide open. He became a sought-after addition at gatherings and parties; most men found him charming and ribald, and women his age found him irresistible. So it was no surprise that he ended up moving in with a wealthy, attractive widow he had known while growing up. Leslie Woodhead-Spikings had a nineteenth century estate outside London that she shared with her grown kids, a menagerie of animals, and a generous, bohemian lifestyle that fit Russell perfectly. She encouraged him to take up his first love when she had known him as a young man—painting—and it stuck. He had always had talent, and now he began doing plein air landscapes that caught the eye of a gallery owner friend, and he was on his way. There would be reasons to return to Africa later in his life, but for now he was quite satisfied to be in a relationship again, to spend his days out painting under the open sky, and to be twenty minutes from Amanda and his twin grandchildren.

He visited Ishi once a year without fail—he was allowed access to the enclosure when the zoo was closing for the night—and when they touched each other, the choice he had made always weighed heavily on him: Was this life better than the almost certain death he would have faced in the wild? Was the look that Ishi gave him each time they met a kind of forgiveness, or was it begging him to take him away from this place, back to where he should have spent the best years of his life, traveling the plains of East Africa with his kind? The elephant couldn't have known the risk he would have faced; that was only known to Russell. Or so he convinced himself.

* * *

With the arrival of Tatiana, Ishi had something to live for again, and he began to come out of his depression. She in turn began to trust another being after what she had witnessed at the end of her time in the Russian circus—she was one of the few survivors that wasn't sold off to private estates for "sport hunting"—and soon they were inseparable, nudging each other around the enclosure and wallowing in their new pond like overgrown calves. The keepers were delighted, as were the customers.

Two years later, Tatiana stood in the middle of the yard, her uterus gushing with fluid, and out dropped a newborn female calf. The keepers were taken completely by surprise, and woefully unprepared. An elephant calf had never been born in a British zoo before, and the staff watched dumbstruck as the mother trumpeted loudly and removed the placenta with her trunk, then gently prodded the baby with her feet until it was able to stand. All the while, Ishi stood guard, his trunk swinging back and forth in warning.

There was a photograph on the front page of the Daily Telegraph that Christmas with the newborn and his parents standing in a light snowfall, and the exhibit's railing was three-deep for weeks after that. But neither of the parents' lives was particularly charmed, so the next chapter of their lives was no surprise in the scheme of things.

The newborn was frolicking around the enclosure, to the delight of onlookers, when she slipped and fell into the barrier moat and became stuck fifteen feet below. No one who witnessed the next minutes could forget the anguished cries of the mother as she tried to reach down with her trunk and extract her calf, but the moat was too deep. People shouted for the keepers, who came running. One of them clambered down and tied a rope around the calf's ankle, a truck arrived and winched her out, and the keeper made his escape.

The calf was limping pronouncedly, and since the first rule with elephants is that no one is safe around a disturbed mother, the decision was made to separate Tatiana from her baby in order to treat the injury. Tatiana's favorite female keeper volunteered to lure the calf into the outbuilding, and was waiting for an opportunity to call the baby over when the head keeper—Ishi and Tatiana's one enemy among the staff—stepped into the enclosure on the other side, ostensibly to distract the parents if needed.

Tatiana was busy attending to her baby when she realized there was a second two-legger behind her. She whirled and saw who it was, saw the bullhook he was wielding, and her ears fanned out in warning. The device was identical to the ones used on her and her sisters in the circus, and they always inflicted pain.

Ishi too was used to this keeper's ways with the bullhook, and knew that to confront him now would lead to disaster. So he stepped in front of Tatiana and trumpeted at the keeper to get out.

Virtually all the witnesses who testified in the following days swore that the bull was trying to prevent further damage as he continued to warn the keeper away, walking purposefully towards him while keeping Tatiana at bay. But when the keeper shouted at Ishi and raised the bullhook, Tatiana had had enough. She slipped around Ishi and charged across the enclosure.

Ishi covered the distance in three quick steps and shoved Tatiana off course, sending her crashing into the barrier. Then he grabbed the keeper with his trunk and hoisted him high in the air, sending the bullhook flying, as Tatiana tried to get at him again. Ishi could have killed him easily, but instead he maneuvered around Tatiana and dropped him into the moat, where Tatiana tried in vain to reach in and be done with him once and for all.

The only footage was from a shaky Sony camcorder that had been turned on halfway through the incident and was filled with horrified screams. The head keeper was adamant that the elephants had tried to kill him and were a danger now and had to be euthanized. But the footage, along with testimony from the other keepers, was enough to cast his version of events into doubt, and it was decided that the elephants would be kept in separate enclosures until they could be sent to other facilities. The mother and baby would be very desirable at another zoo, but to place a possibly dangerous seven-ton bull was going to be difficult.

During the four weeks it took for Tatiana and her calf to be acquired and transferred to the Berlin Zoo, the two elephants stood side by side at the fence that separated their enclosures. They both knew that these were the last days they would be together, and the keepers, with the exception for their unapologetic boss, were moved beyond words.

So Ishi resumed his lonely trek that English winter, the familiar grief he had felt so many times before taking one more piece of his heart. The keepers knew why he had stopped eating again, but they had to keep him alive, the orders were clear on the matter. During the twenty years he was there, they had each come to respect and love him, and even now were unafraid of entering his enclosure.

Parents whispered to their children as they pointed out the "dangerous" elephant they had seen on television; teenagers shouted taunts; old folks met eyes with the beast...and came away confused. He seemed, in their view, simply heartbroken.

Two weeks after Tatiana and her calf had been shipped out, Ishi stood listlessly by the watering hole revisiting a distant memory when he scented something achingly familiar. His hippocampus surged with information, and within seconds he recognized what it was and he looked out at the passing two-leggers.

Amanda had seen the Sheffield Zoo incident on the local news, but was so adamantly against animal captivity that she avoided watching these types of stories; they made her too upset. But this time something piqued her interest; the elephant was being called a hero by witnesses and even his keepers, and the tragedy of losing his mate on top of it made the story extremely intriguing. After much internal debate, she packed her eight-year old twins into her car and took them to a zoo for the first, and hopefully last, time in their lives.

And so it was that she stood at the railing, lifting her girls so they could get a clear view of the mighty bull, when she realized the elephant was moving towards them. It stopped at the edge of the moat, maybe twenty feet away, raised its trunk and let out a long, plaintive screech that stunned her two daughters. Amanda realized that the gestures he was making were directed at her, that his eyes were beseeching hers—and then it hit her who this elephant was. The faint, raised scar on his forehead, the patterns on his ears, the kindness in his eyes, left no doubt.

"Ishi?!" she shrieked, and her daughters and the other visitors all stared in astonishment.

The elephant reached out with his trunk and flapped his ears in delight, then went trotting around the yard before returning, his head tilting from side to side, urine steaming as it splashed on the cold ground. Amanda was so overcome, so in shock, that she had to be restrained from climbing over the railing to reach him.

"Ishi, what are you *doing* here?" she exclaimed. Then, to the onlookers who were holding her back—"I know this elephant! I helped raise him! Let me go!" Her daughters didn't know what to think. Had their mother gone mad?

Within moments a zookeeper appeared and ascertained that this woman and this elephant definitely had a prior relationship, and radioed the office to send for more authority. But before the boss got there, the keeper, a 37-year old Scot named Curtice Horsely, made an astute connection.

"Miss, do you by chance know Russell Hathaway, the old white hunter?"

Amanda stared at him in disbelief. How did this man know her father? How was this all happening? She finally found the words.

"Yes. He's my dad…"

"Come with me then, Miss, let's get you and your daughters somewhere we can talk."

He led them around the back of the compound, unlocked a steel mesh gate and escorted them up a tunnel to the old brick outbuilding. Amanda was having difficulty understanding his thick brogue in the tunnel.

"…comes here about every year or so, I'd say, and the staff allow him into the exhibit after closing. It's quite special to see." He smiled, just as the Head Keeper arrived in an electric cart.

"Sir, this is Amanda Hathaway, Mr. Hathaway's daughter. Amanda, this is Sean McCaffrey, our head zookeeper." They took each other in as they shook hands, and Amanda got the immediate impression that this man would take some handling. She had seen snippets of him on the news, but up close she saw that he had the face of a decades-long alcoholic and eyes that withheld a great store of anger. A sick feeling shot through her; had this man ever mistreated Ishi?

Horsely was still speaking.

"…and she knows our Ishi as well. I thought we might consider letting her visit him through the barrier fence."

McCaffrey grunted and shook his head.

"I'm sorry, Miss, but I can't allow you to go near that elephant. Only our trained keepers can interact with him."

"I understand your concerns completely, Mr. McCaffrey." She saw the look on Horsely's face—he didn't agree, but he had to hold his tongue. Amanda took her daughters' hands and said, "Thank you for your time," and started to usher them out. At the tunnel's entrance, she turned back to McCaffrey. She'd pulled this manuever many times over the years.

"I gather you're trying to move him somewhere else. I might have a solution. Since my father is allowed in to see him, I have a proposal. I'm going to call my paper—I write for the Guardian—and have a film crew come up here with my dad to shoot a piece on Ishi. I'll wager I can get him placed in a preserve in the U.S. within a few days after the piece runs. Take him off your hands. What do you say?"

McCaffrey considered for a moment, wondering if she was just a bullshitter. Even if it came from outside the usual channels, her offer would solve a major problem for him—he didn't like this elephant, and the elephant clearly didn't like him.

"We've always appreciated your dad's gift, so anything that could help us place him somewhere would be quite welcome."

"Your dad's gift." There it was, the confirmation she had feared: her father had indeed taken Ishi from Africa and sent him here without telling anyone in their family. This was such a betrayal, she would have to process it for awhile before she contacted him. But for now she needed to play her last card with the zookeeper.

"Mr. McCaffrey, I raised Ishi as a baby, I've known him for years. Better than my dad, possibly. I'll sign whatever waiver you need, but I'd like to spend a few moments with him before we drive back to London. On the other side of a fence, if that's what you require."

As if on cue, Ishi let out a low, plaintive rumble from his enclosure. He was clearly trying to communicate with Amanda, even McCaffrey could hear it. He thought for a moment, sighed, and nodded at Horsely.

"Stay here with her family. I'll open the paddock and see if he comes over to the fence."

"Thank you, Mr. McCaffrey," said Amanda, "you've made our day. And probably his."

Her daughters were beside themselves with exhilaration as their mother followed McCaffrey through the back gate. Even Amanda's heart raced with anticipation; it had been twenty-three years since she'd last laid eyes on Ishi. He was now a fully-grown bull elephant, not a sweet, innocent adolescent anymore. Would he be gentle with her? Might he be aggressive? He had been basically imprisoned for the last twenty years; what effect would that have on his behavior?

As soon as Amanda stepped into the paddock, Ishi appeared on the other side of the ten-foot high barrier and pressed his head to it. There was just enough room between the bars for him to slip his trunk through.

"Be very careful, Miss," warned McCaffrey from behind her, "he can do a lot of damage if he grabs hold of you."

She didn't respond to McCaffrey beyond a curt nod as she approached the fence.

Ishi reached out and gently touched her. She ran her hands up and down his trunk, caressing his face and whispering as the elephant sniffed his old friend with the orange crown. But her crown was no longer orange. Like him, she was no longer young and spry.

"Oh, Ishi, I am so, so sorry," Amanda whispered as she stared into his right eye, which he had pressed against the bars at her level so he could be as close to her as possible. His "voice" rumbled deep in his throat. Amanda could hardly see through her tears, but she never stopped holding his gaze.

"I will get you out of here, I promise. You'll have a wonderful new home, with no cages and no enemies. You can spend the rest of your days in peace. I promise you, old friend…"

Her daughters watched in amazement as the elephant and their mother held each other through the bars. Horsely was grinning, but he too had tears in his eyes.

* * *

"Were you ever going to tell me?" asked Amanda softly when her father answered the phone late the next night. She had made peace with the idea that he had had the best intentions, even if Ishi's life was arguably not worth living for the last twenty years. There were only the two of them left now: To be strident and judgmental with the only remaining member of her family was not something she would do. The damage she could inflict might be irreversible. No, she would forgive him.

"I've thought of telling you a thousand times," he said after a long silence. "I'm sorry you had to hear about it this way."

"At least I heard about it. Did you ever tell mum?"

"Just before she passed."

"How'd she take it?"

"Like you. She didn't agree with it, but she understood." Amanda didn't respond. "There was no good choice, you know. At least he's alive, and we can send him somewhere fitting for however long he has left."

"I know. I'm already working on it."

"That's the spirit." His daughter heard the catch in his voice, but he tried to hide it anyway. "As always, you're the best, sweetie."

Chapter Twenty-One

Zambia and Kenya, 1999-2002

Kamau sat beside the lone window of the giant cargo jet's aft section as it descended bumpily through rain clouds on final approach to Lusaka International Airport. Behind him, Ishi dozed in his container, but he was starting to show signs of coming around from the sedative. He would not remember much of the journey from England, certainly not as much as he remembered of the ocean voyage twenty years before, and that was okay. This trip would take a mere thirty hours—as opposed to six long, torturous weeks.

After the incident at Sheffield Zoo, Kamau had introduced Amanda to the owners of a private preserve in Florida where Ishi would fit perfectly. The owners were always happy to take any animals from Salisbury that couldn't be released in the wild for whatever reason.

The arrangements for Ishi's transfer to Florida were in the final stages when an offer from the representative of a wealthy benefactor was forwarded to Russell and Amanda in a late night fax.

The owners of Sheffield Zoo had been apprised that there was a private preserve in Zambia that would offer Ishi the ideal situation for an older bull elephant. The preserve was ninety square miles of savanna and forests that had been stocked with hundreds of endangered animals and was protected from poachers by a high, electrified fence and a staff of armed rangers. The most compelling argument was that there was a bachelor herd that had just lost its leader, an old bull who had died of natural causes. They needed another mature bull to keep the pecking order intact and show the herd the ways of the world. Even better, there were dozens of females that Ishi would have his pick of. What better life could they offer him, thought both Russell and Amanda. Amanda did the necessary research on Werner Brandeis and his beneficence to wild animals, and they and the zoo quickly agreed. East Africa—its climate, its flora, its familiarity—and this situation—were even more perfect than a park in Florida. Ishi would be returned to the continent where he belonged.

I am obviously dreaming this. I am staring at several young bulls who are staring back at me, and the orb is hot and bright again like it was before the cold place. And there is no barrier around me—only open, grassy savanna and trees that seem to go on forever.

In my dream, my old two-legger friend is standing beside me. He has been by my side for a while now, as he was by my side many times in my youth. I have the impression that he's ready to leave me again, but that is as it should be: I can't keep watch over him out here forever. When I wake up, I expect he'll be gone.

Kamau got back in the transport truck with the preserve's game-keeper, a retired warden from Zambezi National Park, and watched as Ishi ambled toward the treeline, then turned back to see if the young bulls were following him. They were. He let out a low rumble only they could hear, and the little bachelor herd picked up its pace and caught him as he disappeared into the trees. Kamau beamed, and the warden nodded.

"This should work out splendidly then," he said as he started up the truck, whistled for his two rangers to climb back in, and turned towards home. For Kamau, this trip had been one of the happiest of his life. When he'd heard that Ishi was alive and well and in an English zoo, and that he would be accompanying him back to Africa, he literally dropped the hallway phone's receiver and had to sit down. The pangs of sadness he had felt every time he pictured his old friend reduced to a pile of bones were now gone, replaced by an ebullience he hadn't felt in years.

I think of Big Black often these days, and try my best to be as good a stew-ard to my young friends as he was to me. Without the sharp temper, I hope, but you'll have to ask them.

I have walked this new place for days now, and I taste and scent every tree and watering hole as if I was a young calf again. I miss Tatiana profoundly, but that is all I miss of the cold place. I have even shown affection for the plains- and tree-dwellers I've met here, and I can tell they are appreciative of it. I have met no rival yet, so I am the most respected and feared creature around—except for the two-leggers, of course.

Today I encountered a barrier fence for the first time, and it stretched as far as I could walk. I asked my young friends about it, and they said it has been here ever since they arrived. It goes on for days and it is dangerous; it stings badly if touched, and the wound it leaves hurts much like that of a big cat's claws. It must be avoided.

As much as I am grateful to be in this new place, there is something missing. The loneliness I always felt in the cold place, the pit in my stomach that left me feeling heavy and listless most every waking hour, is disappearing, but it is not completely gone. I am in my old world again, yes, but it is not the same, and I've been pondering why.

I realize now that my old life is still out there—my friends, my aunties, my clans; all the familiar landmarks, the sense that I grew up somewhere, that I belong to a place that has my memories in it. Unlike the night sky in the cold place, the stars here are in their same familiar places, so I feel I must be close to my home. At least close enough. I will make the best of life while I am here, but there is an ache in my bones that tells me I will be moving on one day.

* * *

The same unforeseen changes that ended Kamau's career in the Wildlife Ministry visited someone else as well. Gichinga Kimathi was a Kikuyu too, so when the new president's Karenji chief of staff and his transition team called Gichinga in for an assessment, the man looked up from Gichinga's personnel file with a soft whistle and a mirthless smile.

"My, my, Mr. Kamathi… We are extremely impressed with your collection rates. None of us has never seen such high rates before. How, might we ask, have you been so successful?"

Gichinga knew before he answered that the jig was up. Apparently some of his staff had been interviewed in the days before, and he knew now that they had not been kind about his leadership or his methods. Gichinga had never risen to the status he felt he deserved, and these new fools were either going to demote him or fire him, so he made a quick, bold decision. He stood up without a word, smiled coolly, and walked out the door. He had better ways to make a living, he told himself as he walked down the hall, and he was going to pursue them, starting immediately.

His son Mutegi Kimathi was now twenty-three and the spitting image of his father in looks and temperament. When you are raised by a cold, demanding father who you've witnessed abusing your kind, devoted mother, you either stand up to him—or succumb. Or stand up to him the first time at age ten, get beaten, and then succumb, which was the case with Mutegi. His anger as he grew older was perhaps even more profound than his father's; he'd been expelled from two schools for fighting. Now he worked for his father in a profession that required no diploma, just the right connections and a bit of on-the-job training. And a crew.

Gichinga had taken him on several poaching missions and set him up with his buyers, and Mutegi was now quite proficient, especially since poachers had gravitated to using fully automatic rifles. Their prey never stood a chance; entire herds were slaughtered in mere seconds.

So when Mutegi and two of his crew were arrested by the Field Force in a sting operation just outside the border of Tsavo, Mutegi spent three weeks in a foul, overcrowded jail. His fine was mysteriously paid and he found his father waiting for him on the teeming street outside.

Gichinga was finally through with government, he told his son over a bottle of celebratory rum in their favorite illicit bar, and he wanted to re-establish their "business" as partners.

"I have a plan to increase our profits many times over."

"And how is that?"

"We sell directly to the Chinese. Cut the government middle-men out."

Mutegi stared at his father, taking all the ramifications in. "It will be risky—we won't have protection if we are ever caught."

"What did our 'protection' do for you this last time?"

Mutegi looked past him at the strippers parading their wares on the stage and shrugged. He had no answer.

His father continued. "I will be coming with you again. We'll work together, father and son. Like old times. We will be richer than we ever imagined."

Mutegi could see how serious his father was about the plan. Finally he nodded.

"Okay. Let's try it."

Gichinga put his arm around his son's shoulders and grinned.

"Good. We start tomorrow."

As his father predicted, they would soon be richer than they ever imagined. But no matter how much money you have, sometimes things just don't work out like you planned.

CHAPTER TWENTY-TWO

Tanzania, Present Day

ONCE THE ELEPHANT WAS past Lake Tanganyika and had entered the tribal areas two days later, the local human celebrants dropped away, leaving Westbrook and his director, a noted National Geographic documentary filmmaker, to follow Ishi in peace. They were now using a rotation of mini-drones that had been donated to them by a new company called GoPro as the first civilian UAVs were coming on the market. They could follow at an unobtrusive height and distance, and most wildlife paid them little attention, though occasionally a large, irritated bird would attack one and leave them blind until they could send another drone aloft. The crew was now able to dispense with the ground-based cameras and the helicopter, which made life much easier for everyone.

Ishi soon realized it was no coincidence that a strange, faintly-buzzing "bird" showed up every morning and trailed him until it, or one of its brethren, departed at nightfall. And the way they moved and hovered was like no bird he'd ever seen. The old bull was no fool: He knew his two-legger friends were still out there, watching him.

Then something unexpected happened. One sundown as Ishi started out for his night's journey, he came upon a herd of two extended families—a dozen females of varying ages with their young calves and pre-adolescent males—who were gathered on the banks of a river. He was prepared to keep his distance, knowing he likely wouldn't be welcome in their midst, when the matriarch walked up to him without fear and scented him up and down with her trunk. Then she looked into his eyes and greeted him with a gentle murmur.

"You appear to be on a long journey, stranger. Is your destination far from here?"

Ishi was taken aback, not so much by her directness or her keen perception, which were typical of older matriarchs, but by the tenderness in her voice. No female except Tatiana had been so solicitous since he'd been a mature bull—and that situation had been an unnatural, forced relationship. He regarded the matriarch with equal kindness.

"I am on my way back to my birthplace, kind elder, and yes, it is far from here. Are you acquainted with the giant mountain with snow on its crown?"

"I have heard of it, but I have never seen it. It is said to be many horizons away." She had placed her trunk near his mouth. "You have the scent of a wound on your breath. Are you strong enough to make a journey like this?"

"I will get there."

By now the other members of the herd had approached, sensing from their matriarch that Ishi was no danger. The males looked up at him in awe; he was as big a bull as any of them had ever seen. Two older sisters scented the site of his wound and looked at him with concern.

"This was made by the two-leggers, was it not?" asked one of them.

Ishi reluctantly began to explain, but that just opened him up to more questions, and pretty soon he'd told them the entire story of his journey so far. The herd was fascinated, and by twilight he was friends with every one of them. Finally the matriarch, whose name was Deep Waters, signaled the clan for silence.

"I want to ask our new friend if he would like to travel with us for a while," she said to her clan, then looked at Ishi. "We are headed in the same direction as you, and we know the best routes. We will provide you with companionship, and you can offer us protection from unforeseen dangers until we part company. Would you like that?"

Ishi knew that they didn't need his protection—the matriarch was just offering a kindness. And then a flood of powerful, pent up emotions poured out of him. His feelings were so apparent that the females all took turns comforting him. This was a type of bull they had rarely encountered, and they were all now committed to taking him as far as they could.

In his trailer, Jeremy Westbrook watched the feed from the drone with great interest. As the herd escorted their new friend into the darkness, and the drone was recalled for the night, he texted Rebecca and their director with the news. This could be a new wrinkle, they all realized—and not necessarily a bad one.

CHAPTER TWENTY-THREE

England, New York, Kenya and Zambia, 2003-2011

As in any family when a son or daughter has been taken early, the grief is cataclysmic. It lessens with time but never goes away; the parents must learn to live with broken hearts for the rest of their lives.

A sibling's grief is enormous too, but in a different way. For Amanda, she carried Terence with her as a ghost who resided in her as she lived her life. If she saw something extraordinary—a meteor shower while in the mountains of Kandahar, for instance, or standing onstage during the climax of a U2 concert—she would share it with him as if he were there with her, even speaking aloud to him. It never struck her as odd, living for the two of them. Even though she was skeptical about an afterlife, she carried him with her as a fellow traveler for the rest of her days.

Amanda eventually tired of the traveling that her investigative assignments required and, as a single mother, cut back her duties so she could raise her daughters properly. She never considered sending them off to boarding school—she'd learned that lesson—and on the rare occasions when she had to go off on a story, she would drop her twins with Russell and Leslie, where they were doted on and usually begged to stay when she came back to collect them. Truth be told, Russell was a much better grandfather than he'd been a father. He had finally learned his lessons.

Amanda had started writing nonfiction books in her late thirties, and was now receiving modest advances from a boutique publisher. Her history with men had pretty much cured her of wanting anything more than friendship with them, and by her late forties she had made enough of a life—with her family, her work and her friends—to keep her busy and relatively happy. When her girls went off to university she took the occasional lover, but they always ended up reminding her why she was alone.

When the events of 9/11 blew away the short, peaceful sleep that had settled over the West after the Cold War ended, Amanda was torn whether to return to her job as a full-time journalist at the age of fifty-one or to stay on the sidelines and contribute in some other way. Having started going through the change of life, she decided it was a young woman's game, and was looking around for opportunities when she learned that her banishment from the United States was no longer in effect; the laws had been modified in the intervening years, and she could apply for a visa at any time.

She was walking the streets of Lower Manhattan three weeks later, and though she and New York had changed in profound ways, it was like a lifelong friendship that you picked up where you'd left off. After walking around the ruins of Ground Zero for several days she had an idea for a book, an incendiary series of essays and interviews—with scholars, politicians, generals, Islamic clerics—that dealt with the approaching, possibly generations-long battle of civilizations. One year later, "The Coming War—A Clash of Centuries," landed on the New York Times nonfiction best seller list in its fifth week of publication.

On the promotional tour, she gave scores of interviews, but didn't mention why she hadn't returned to America before now. That part of her past was not a secret she wanted to divulge. She was sitting in a midtown Manhattan Hilton hotel suite during lunch break when a man appeared in her doorway without the usual PR representative to announce him.

"Excuse me, Ms. Hathaway? I don't have an appointment to see you, but I think you might like to have a conversation anyway..."

Her blood ran cold when she realized who was standing in front of her. Thirty years had changed Ariel Levine profoundly as well. He was like a faded copy of the picture she had of him in her memory. The anger he'd possessed as a young man was gone, replaced by an almost eerie calm. He sat down in the chair opposite her, looked into her stunned eyes, and smiled disarmingly.

"You don't need to worry, I stopped hating you years ago. I actually came here to apologize."

Amanda stared. His words, and the sentiment, pierced thirty years of armor so completely that she felt like she was in that high meadow again, in that courtroom again, betraying him.

"Why…would you want to apologize to me? By rights, I should be apologizing to you."

He shook his head slowly.

"No, what you did saved me. I didn't realize it at the time…but it did. Even if you didn't intend it." He looked down. "Doing time can really change you, if you let it. If you don't let the bitterness get to you."

"It certainly seems to have changed you… What about the others, where are they? Geoffrey…Cajun Sammy…?"

"I didn't really follow anyone else's fate that closely. Except Max's," he smiled sadly. "And yours. From the papers at first, then on the internet. You've done really well for yourself. I'm happy for you."

Amanda was taken aback.

"Thank you." She noticed a gold wedding band. "I see you're married—well, I'm assuming that. Do you have a family?"

"I do. Like you. But my wife and I are separated."

"I'm sorry to hear that. I know the pain."

He looked out the windows at the Manhattan skyline, and she took in his profile. He was in good shape for an American in his mid-fifties, his body only slightly thickened, his hair still full and dark. He looked back at her.

"I found something while I was inside that saved me. I became a Buddhist, of all things."

He was about the last person she would have thought could find comfort in spiritualism. She was about to say this when her PR rep walked in with a new interviewer.

"Ms. Hathaway, this is Alice Marsden from the Detroit Free—" Realizing there was another visitor in the room, she stopped. "I'm so sorry, I didn't realize…"

Ariel stood up from his chair quickly.

"Please, I was just leaving." He had addressed the PR rep, but his eyes never left Amanda's. "Thank you so much for your time, Ms. Hathaway. It was a pleasure."

He smiled at the two new arrivals as he skirted around them. Amanda just watched as he walked out the door—and then a powerful urge grabbed her, and she bolted to her feet.

"I'm sorry, Ms. Marsden," she said to the interviewer. "I don't mean to be rude, but would you mind waiting here for just a minute? I need to talk to that gentleman for a moment longer."

She smiled politely and ducked out the door. She caught Ariel as he was approaching the elevators in an adjacent corridor.

"Hang on," she called. "You didn't think you could get away with just walking out the door like that after thirty years, did you?"

He looked surprised, then realized she was smiling, and broke into one himself.

"Wow. No, that was a little chickenshit, wasn't it?"

"Maybe. But it took a lot of courage to find me and show up. Give yourself credit."

He laughed, and they both felt the past slipping away. Or, rather, creeping back up on them.

"You're right," he said, "it took a bit of…talking to myself."

"I've learned to be a little forward in my advanced age. If you truly want something, you have to ask for it."

He shook his head in wonder.

"I'm glad to see you turned out to be such an evolved human being. Though I can't say I'm surprised."

"I've got a million questions. Do you have dinner plans?" she blurted, surprising herself as much as Ariel. "There's a nice restaurant around the corner, give me your number and I'll call you when I'm done here."

They couldn't look away from each other. They both knew exactly what was happening.

When Amanda awoke the next morning to a shaft of sunlight slicing through her hotel room's curtains, she looked over and saw Ariel asleep on his side, his well-kept physique peeking through the thrashed bed-sheets, and smiled with the memory of their lovemaking. Very little had changed in the intervening years, she thought, except they couldn't go several times a night; their appetites had dimmed after one orgasm. But considering the mileage they'd both put on, they were doing pretty well. After all these years, he was still the best lover she'd ever had.

He was a horse trainer in upstate New York, appropriately; he'd gone to school after serving eight years at the Hudson Correctional Facility, met with the state board of licensing when he was released and landed a job through a Buddhist friend at a thoroughbred outfit in Saratoga. There wasn't much money in it, but there aren't many high-paying professions when you've done serious time. Amanda's heart went out to him: he would have made a great veterinarian if things had gone differently, but he accepted his fate without complaint, and his dignity was never compromised.

She ran her hand down his hip lightly and he stirred. She reached over and caressed his lower abdomen…and he moaned. Moments later he was inside her, and they had a sweet, slow climax to begin the day.

They both knew they had no future together—this had been about healing the wounds of the past—so everything had come easily and openly. The best gift of all, for Amanda, was that she could finally forgive herself, could stop paying for her greatest transgression, her greatest regret. He was okay now, she saw; the fates had been righted, and they could keep the secret of their past between just the two of them.

After breakfast they walked the few blocks to Grand Central Station together. They promised to keep in touch, and, after a last kiss, Ariel boarded his train.

Though they reconnected on Facebook when it came out a few years later, and followed each other's lives from a distance, they never saw each other again.

* * *

For a male Caucasian to reach the age of seventy-five without any major health issues is rare. Like most of his generation, Russell had smoked, eaten a high fat diet and drunk plenty of alcohol, and his mother had had a history of heart disease. So it should have come as no surprise when, one day while painting by himself on the moor a few miles north of Leslie's estate, he felt a slight dizziness, ignored it, and then a paralyzing headache rocked him so hard he wanted to scream, but nothing came out. He watched from a vantage point outside his body as his paint brush froze on the canvas, then slipped from his fingers. He leaned down to pick it up—and collapsed into his easel. He rolled over and looked up at the sky as his symptoms kept spiraling, and realized with a terrible certainty what was happening. He'd treated clients for strokes in the bush, and he knew he needed to get medication quickly or he would be left a paraplegic in a wheelchair—never able to paint again, never able to be Leslie's lover again, never able to play with his grandchildren again. He could not allow this fate to befall him.

So with every ounce of his training and strength he stumbled, then crawled, to his Land Rover parked a hundred meters away on a dirt path. He could barely turn the key in the ignition, couldn't even lift his left arm, and realized that driving to the main road was out of the question. So he did the only thing he could think of—he hit the horn repeatedly in a rhythm that would notify anyone within hearing to seek out the source. If they had been Scouts or military they would recognize it as Morse code for SOS.

He had no idea how much time had passed when he heard a tractor engine rumbling faintly, getting closer. It was drizzling by now, and Russell was laying across the front seat with his right hand feebly sounding the horn every few seconds. The left side of his face and his left arm were drooping or useless. He was preparing to give in to a long, peaceful sleep when he was lifted roughly and someone was shouting in his face.

The farmer, an ex-paratrooper, had heard the horn as he drove past on the main road. He had jumped down from his tractor and ascertained that Russell couldn't move or speak, then hauled him into the Land Rover's passenger seat and buckled him in. Driving as fast on a rain-slicked country road as possible, he reached the local clinic in under five minutes.

As fate would have it, an exceedingly bright Indian resident was on duty that afternoon and recognized that Russell was having an ischemic stroke, quickly gave him an IV of Alteplase and a dose of aspirin. A stricken Leslie met the ambulance out front a few minutes later and followed it to Royal Brompton Hospital in London, where Russell was stabilized in the ICU.

By morning, Amanda and Leslie were apprised by the hospital's chief neurologist that Russell had been extremely lucky; he had gotten treatment just in time, and he would probably have no mental impairment. With physical therapy he might possibly even regain full use of his left hand.

The farmer and the clinic doctor had been put there by angels, Leslie proclaimed, and over a dinner she threw for them several weeks later, she donated 10,000 pounds to a college fund for each of their children. To say that Russell had found another great woman with whom to share his life would have been a gross understatement.

* * *

By all rights I should be as content as any creature alive. I have the sun on my back again and my belly is full. I have many friends, and several females who desire my company from time to time. Even the two-leggers here are kind and respectful.

But this place is somehow a strange, contained version of the larger world; I have roamed it for days at a time, and no matter how far I go, I always pass the same landmarks and eventually end up in the place I started. Even the absence of danger seems unnatural; the big cats seem cautious and beaten, like the animals I observed in the cold place. After several seasons of this, it has begun to wear on me, and the impulse to leave has grown too big to ignore. The young bulls are almost ready to live on their own now, so I have been planning my escape. I will be gone soon.

* * *

Poaching in Kenya had reached epidemic proportions in the last decade, fueled by gangs of Somali soldiers looking to finance their war to the north with profits from blood ivory. Kamau saw the results of their viciousness up close: orphaned elephants were arriving at Salisbury in tragically high numbers, and the stories of mass killings from his old friends in the Wildlife Service were unspeakable. After checking in on his keepers and their young charges each night, Kamau would wander the grounds of Salisbury like a ghost; even Makena's words of solace could not ease his burden for long. The murder of "his" creatures made him so inconsolable that even his well-known sense of humor had gone missing.

A hundred miles away, a different emotion was at play in a very different man. Gichinga Kimathi was seeing the carnage up close as well, but from another perspective; he, his son and their crew were in direct competition with the Somalis, and they had to keep a sharp eye out for them or they might stumble into a firefight. At sixty years of age, Gichinga was as fit as most forty-year olds, but he hadn't counted on having to dodge the Field Force *and* hopped up, cold-blooded guerrillas. He was getting too old for this, he realized each morning as he left the warmth of his blanket to start a cooking fire instead of enjoying the comforts of his Nairobi apartment. He decided he was going to hand over the business to his son again, no matter how much they were pulling down. And this time for good.

CHAPTER TWENTY-FOUR

Zambia, Present Day (Nine Weeks Earlier) and England and Kenya

I HAVE MADE THE DECISION *to carry out my plan. The rainy season, which I marked as the best time to begin my journey, has just arrived. I will have plenty of food and water and less chance of running into two-leggers, who usually seek shelter during the rains. I will have the nights to myself.*

My young friends have followed me to a far corner of our world, where I have picked out the ideal place. They have agreed to help me escape and then return to their usual grazing spots, in hopes that the two-leggers will not notice that I have gone.

The strongest of them have taken turns uprooting a large tree, which I have ascertained will fall directly on the fence, crushing it. And in a thunderous crash it has done just that. I now approach the flattened barrier to sense if there is still an aura emanating from it.

No! It is dead, and I have only to walk out!

The old elephant turned back to the young bulls watching behind him, but none spoke. Ishi realized it was incumbent upon him, and he began with his gravest, sage bull tone:

"I regret you cannot go with me, my young friends, but you will leave here when it is your time." None of them said a word; some couldn't even look at him. "We have had a good many rainy seasons together, and I will remember our times as among the best of my life. You are all going to be fine bulls, and you will prosper beautifully without me. So let me go before I change my mind."

They converged on him in an emotional twining of trunks and clacking of tusks, pushing up against him as they intoned their goodbyes. Ishi did everything he could to not show his sadness; in the end he was glad it was drizzling so they could not see his tears.

He turned and picked his way carefully over the fallen fence, then started trotting as he entered the trees he would use as cover from now on. He didn't look back, trying to show his young friends the emotional strength of a powerful bull. Like Big Black surely would have done.

Three weeks later, after traveling almost exclusively at night and avoiding all human habitation, the big bull was crossing a rain-slicked hardscape where the false beasts ran when he made a careless mistake. He had not been able to keep his intake of food up—the nubs of his teeth hurt too much whenever he chewed—and his constant hunger affected his focus. So his mind was elsewhere when a pair of headlights appeared out of the rain, racing right at him. He froze, then started to back up as the false beast spun violently. It stopped just short of him, now very quiet, and he saw the face of the two-legger inside. His eyes were as big as a lemur's. The elephant held the two-legger's gaze for a moment, realized he was fine, and then continued across the barrier.

A thought occurred to him as he disappeared into the darkness on the other side. This was the first two-legger he'd encountered since he'd left the preserve. Might this two-legger tell his friends what he had just seen?

Six weeks later, several guests were finishing a raucous Sunday dinner in Leslie's main dining room when the phone rang in a distant hall. Moments later Russell was called to the phone. It was Amanda, and she had news.

"They want us to fly down and get to Salisbury right away. They're expecting him to arrive in the area within the week."

Russell was thrilled for a moment, then perplexed. At 87 he was still fairly sharp most of the time, but something vexed him about this piece of information.

"They're paying for this whole show, right?"

Amanda smiled to herself.

"I don't know anything about that, Dad. I put the tickets on your card." She heard a plaintive exclamation from his end and felt terrible. "Dad, I'm joking. Of course they're paying; you're the star of the show, remember?"

"Well, after Ishi. And you, naturally. And let's not forget Kamau."

"Oh, we won't. He's getting our old rooms ready as we speak."

Russell grunted his approval. He still painted, but only on the estate's grounds. This didn't concern him, since he was now painting from memory anyway. The clearest region of his memory—African landscapes.

Amanda was speaking again, he realized.

"Oh, I haven't told you the best part. We're meeting Mr. Brandeis at Heathrow tomorrow morning. He's flying us down on his private jet."

"Well, I'll be gobsma—" He stopped, unsure of something. "This isn't a joke too, is it?"

"No Dad, it's for real. And I'm sorry I pulled your leg." She was speaking as a daughter who was really more a caretaker now. "They're sending a car for us, so I'll pick you up at half past nine, okay? Tell Leslie to pack you for a spot of rain, it's still wet season."

At the same time, roughly sixty miles south of the giant, snow-capped volcano that had loomed in the distance for three days, Ishi and Deep Waters and her clan were laying up for the night in a forest of mango trees. They'd been traveling without haste, skirting Lake Eyasi and then Ngorongoro Crater, because Ishi could now only cover about ten miles a day. The females didn't mind; they took turns telling the stories of their lives, though they all knew that the most interesting life by far was Ishi's. He had been places and seen things none of them could have ever conceived of.

Except for the rains, which sometimes grounded the drones, Westbrook and the film crew had had a relatively uneventful time following the elephant and his new escorts. There had been the occasional standoff with other bulls, but Ishi was big enough, and could still adopt a dangerous enough attitude, that they didn't challenge him. When a hot-headed adolescent attempted to mount a female in their herd, Deep Water's clan decided he wasn't a proper suitor and, with Ishi providing the necessary persuasion, drove him off. Any farms or villages on their route were paid for whatever crops were damaged, so there were no serious confrontations with angry humans.

Though the area ahead to the Kenyan border looked benign from the air, one never knew from day to day. There had been poaching incidents within several miles of their cavalcade for the last two weeks, so the film crew's scouts were being extra vigilant. Just the threat of poachers made the viewing audience nervous with anticipation; the ratings had risen steadily, and were setting records for virtually every cable channel that carried the show, as well as a huge online following. Ishi would never know it, but he was probably the most beloved animal in the world at the moment.

The next morning, as the herd gathered for the day and the drone discreetly arrived, Deep Waters walked up to Ishi and stroked his face with her trunk.

"My friend," she said after a moment, "I regret having to tell you this…but my sisters say they have gone far enough. We have seen the great mountain, and we have escorted you as close to your birthplace as we can. It is time for us to return home."

Ishi had been expecting this for a while now, and though he treasured their company, he knew he would have to make the rest of his journey alone.

"There is no need for you to apologize. You have been as good to me as any friends I have ever known."

The other females moved closer now, followed by the young bulls and the calves. Deep Waters' voice became heavy with emotion.

"You are one of a kind, Ishi. We will never forget you." Ishi pressed his forehead to hers as she continued. "Your heart is big, my friend. I doubted this when we first met you—but you will finish your journey, no matter how far you have to go."

The herd pressed in and each member touched Ishi, most of them too moved to say anything. Once again, it was Ishi who had to find the strength to move on, to leave another set of friends behind.

He started walking up a boulder-studded hill. Then the females turned and started walking back toward their faraway home. The drone followed Ishi, and just as he crested the rise, it swung around and picked up the herd as they turned, raised their trunks, and gave a long, plaintive chorus of shrieks.

What had just occurred was not lost on Westbrook as he watched the feed. These creatures were so profoundly sentient that even humans would have trouble rivaling their feelings. He and the director would save this moment for the climax of tomorrow's broadcast. They anticipated, correctly, that the viewing audience would be dumbstruck.

Two evenings later, Ishi had left the majestic mountain behind as it towered over the still-sunlit clouds, and was walking alone through a thinned-out forest when a faint scent reached him from somewhere far off. It disappeared for a moment, then returned on the breeze with a clear and powerful presence. For some unknown reason it frightened him, and he stood stock still, trunk raised, trying to identify where he knew it from.

The olfactory system in humans can summon memories from deep in the unconscious, sometimes even more potently than the other senses. In mammals like elephants, it is even more compelling, since quickly distinguishing scents can be a matter of life and death. This was a two-legger smell, mixed with the smoke from a cooking fire and the aroma of burned animal flesh. But what was the overriding odor? What was it that had unsettled him so?

Suddenly it hit him and his heart seemed to plummet. A memory started flooding out of his unconscious; it was so vivid that it transported him back to a grassy meadow with his mother and his birth herd feeding all around him. He could see and hear everything; his mother looking up with intense concentration, sensing danger; his aunties surrounding him and his fellow calves; then boom sticks exploding all around them, and the horror of seeing his mother fall, his sisters fall, their voices calling in agony and shock. And then he was alone, and there was an overpowering stench of blood.

He came back to the present for a moment and stood there in the growing darkness, his emotions swirling violently. This was the event he had forgotten all those years ago, he realized; this was the missing piece that had somehow disappeared from his memory…until the scent on the breeze awakened it.

He closed his eyes and returned to the past, to live out the last moments in case the memory eluded him again. He was staring up at a two-legger who had been busy bloodying his mother's face. He touched the killer, who turned around to face him, and Ishi let loose a torrent of urine—he couldn't tell if it was now or fifty years ago—because looking into those eyes was like looking at death. And that was what Ishi wanted—to die right there beside his mother. So without fearing any consequences, he charged the two-legger, and the memory abruptly ended.

Ishi stood there in the present, his heart thumping in his chest. He recognized the scent now, and the two-legged killer who owned it. There was no doubt. And he was here somewhere, all these years later, somewhere upwind of him.

Gichinga's son Mutegi and his crew had had one too many run-ins with the Somalis to work the Tsavo area any longer. Mutegi had broken an ankle while fleeing a platoon of hair-triggered Somalis three weeks earlier and was temporarily out of commission, so Gichinga had taken his place to track a big herd that was making its way south along the Kenya-Tanzania border. With no guerrillas and no Field Force to deal with in the area, Gichinga and crew were feeling relaxed as they polished off their rum and crashed for the night. With any luck, tomorrow morning they would have their ivory and be heading home by lunchtime.

Gichinga was by nature a light sleeper—this trait had kept him alive several times over—so his eyes popped open at a distinctive smell that was all around him. In the moonlight he saw a dark shape above him blotting out the stars, and he realized what the smell was.

Elephant.

He started to throw his blanket off and reach for his weapon when a powerful force pinned him down and stifled any cry. In fact his lungs suddenly couldn't get any oxygen and his eyes bulged dangerously. He looked up at the beast as his brain scrambled to make sense of what was happening. And in its eyes he saw not a crazed rogue elephant, but a calm, solemn presence taking him in. Unhurried, even—and Gichinga realized why when he glimpsed his fellow poachers' unmoving bodies lying beside their blankets around the embers of the fire. This can't be happening, his brain managed to think, and he begged desperately for this all to be just a bad dream.

But he was very much awake, and suddenly he was being picked up and flung violently into the air. As he spun like a ragdoll he saw he was higher than the surrounding trees—and knew there was going to be a hard landing. He slammed down awkwardly in a lava field, shattering multiple bones in his legs, arms, and ribcage. He tried to leap up and make an escape, but all he could do was gasp.

The beast's trunk picked him up again, slowly swinging him back and forth as it walked over and dropped him by the fire. Gichinga moaned as the initial shock lifted and the pain of his injuries started to hit him. He spit up blood, and knew instinctively that this was where it was all going to end.

"What did I do to deserve this?" he rasped painfully. "Do…we know each other?"

Ishi just stared, but Gichinga had the strange sense that the elephant knew what he was asking. Ishi seemed to answer—by pressing a tusk into Gichinga's abdomen until he howled in agony.

"Ayyyeee! Ayyeee…"

The elephant released the pressure and Gichinga vomited up blood, which froze him in such agony he couldn't make a sound. He lay back, took a last gasping breath, and spat at the elephant.

The beast slapped Gichinga's head violently with his trunk. Then he reared up and brought his full weight down on him like a house, and Gichinga's insides exploded out of every orifice in his body.

The elephant stared down at his old nemesis, who was clearly not going to take breath again. Ishi had hurt very few creatures in his life—and then only when he'd been provoked—and he'd never killed any, certainly not two-leggers. So what he'd just done gave him a strange, unrecognizable feeling. Something dark seeped from his heart. It wasn't guilt, or regret, which are human constructs, but something more elemental. The fates had been righted; the end of this two-legger's life, and of his friends, had been his duty. His victims would never harm any of his brothers or sisters again; this was as it should be. He decided he would not think of it further. He turned and calmly walked away from the dying fire, heading back toward his prescribed route.

He met up with a herd at daybreak and greeted them warily as they passed each other. Neither of them was aware that this was the herd the poachers had targeted for death. The fates had indeed been righted.

A few hours later one of the drones found Ishi—they'd been frantically searching for him since he'd taken his side trip the night before—and everyone in the crew was relieved by his reappearance on their "trail." They would not learn until days later of a fatal incident in the border area. From what could be reconstructed from the scavenger-gnawed bones, four poachers had been crushed to death in their sleep, apparently by a rogue elephant. It never occurred to the crew that it could have been their kindly old bull…exacting revenge for the killing of his family fifty-odd years ago.

CHAPTER TWENTY-FIVE

Kenya, Present Day

I<small>F</small> J<small>EAN COULD HAVE SEEN</small> Salisbury Farm she would have thought a safari from the old days was about to go out, Amanda mused sadly as she watched the keepers feeding the orphans their evening meal. Added to the usual chaos of the orphanage, the living quarters were filling up with activity. Westbrook and the film crew were already working out of the four-car garage, where drones were flying in and out every few hours. The staff's quarters were now all occupied by the newcomers: Russell and Leslie, Amanda, and Westbrook and Rebecca who, even with their fifteen-year age disparity, had become a couple through proximity and their shared passion for wildlife. Werner Brandeis, who was so taken by the orphanage that he wanted to fund it the moment he laid eyes on it, had urged Kamau and Makena to remain in the master bedroom, but they had moved into the guest cottage, giving him little choice but to take their bedroom.

Though Kamau rarely drank alcohol, and Amanda rarely drank once she'd hit her fifties, they found a bottle of vintage Port in the liquor cabinet and walked out to the yard after dinner. They talked for hours, laughing and crying as they caught each other up on their lives. Their kids, in their mid-teens to 20s now and trying to negotiate the strange new world on their own, gave them each the most pride—and the most heartache.

"You remember Ndegwa, my old friend from my village?" asked Kamau with a twinkle in his eye. His sense of humor had slowly begun to re-awaken of late.

"Of course. Your walkabout mate. How's he faring these days?"

"He became our tribal chief when his father died a few years ago. He still visits me every year, without fail."

"That's quite a bond you guys have. Especially with the disparity between you culturally. You're lucky."

"That's what I wanted to tell you about. This is hilarious…and heart-breaking." He poured another glass of Port. "Each time I see him, we have less and less in common. It's like talking to an ancient civilization. Try explaining the internet to a man who's never driven a car."

"Aw, that's sad," Amanda said, but then couldn't hide a smile. "At least you're staying in touch with your heritage."

"Are you mocking me, little sister?" He punched her arm playfully. Their affection for each other in their fifties was no different than it had been in their youth.

"So here's the best part. He asked me if my fourteen-year old would like to celebrate the rite of manhood with them, like we did in the old days."

"You mean like the first time we met you?"

"Exactly. He's so sweet and naïve that he thought being circumcised by a village elder and then told to go out into the wild alone for three days and nights would be just the thing for Nzala."

"Aren't you being a little cruel? It's all he knows."

"Am I?" Kamau thought about it for a moment. "The hygiene alone would be dangerous. And he'd be totally lost without his laptop!"

They both laughed at the idea of their kids' generation being appalled by theirs. They grew quiet, staring up at the star-filled African night. Finally Kamau raised his glass.

"Here's to our dear mama, may she rest in peace. And to our dear friend Ishi, who will hopefully be joining us soon."

The old bull had entered Tsavo the day before, the scouts had relayed, and was about four or five days away from Salisbury…if all went well.

I have been gone from this place for most of my life, yet it is still here waiting for me, unchanged. The sights, the sounds, the smells, all bring back memories of my youth as I walk through familiar valleys and bathe in favorite rivers. The faces I meet now are new, and young; sadly, from my queries, all my old friends seem to have passed on. But since I knew that I would find my way here, and I have, there is no doubt that some of them will still be walking the plains when I arrive.

A handsome white egret had befriended Ishi the week before, and rode atop his back picking at the riches left in the mud caking his hide. Ishi didn't even realize it had been there until one evening it spoke to him.

"Kind host, we need to find a flame tree, you have a rotten smell coming from your wound here. I've eaten all the treats that were living there, but your situation is not getting any better."

Ishi was as alarmed that he understood the bird's thoughts as he was at the information the bird proffered. He'd had many egrets travel with him in his day, but none had ever addressed him before.

"You...can speak to me in my language?"

"Well, that begs another question, I'm afraid. Either I have a special gift...or your mental state isn't what it once was."

This alarmed Ishi even more. He had noticed that his focus, and his memory, were slipping in the last few weeks—or was it longer?—and he was starting to see things that, upon further scrutiny, weren't really there. His delirium from the wound was one possible explanation, but in his lucid moments he knew he was fooling himself. This was from getting old. He'd seen it in many elephants as they drew down on their last days. And now it was happening to him. The talking bird was the clearest evidence yet.

But even if he was just talking to himself, he enjoyed the conversation, so he decided to continue it.

"I am looking for others of my kind, but my vision isn't what it once was. Would you be so kind as to fly ahead every now and then and tell me if you see any of my kind? It would make my journey more fruitful, and save a lot of needless searching."

The egret found none of his kind for two days as they made their way north through the hills of southern Tsavo. The next afternoon they came upon a savanna filled with plains-dwellers browsing in the high grass, acutely aware of several big cats lying in the shade of a lone acacia tree. The egret flew off, and a little while later came floating back on a warm draft and lighted between Ishi's shoulders.

"Well, we are in luck. There are a number of your kind just over the horizon. If you wish, I will guide you."

The rainy season had tapered off over the last weeks, but there was still a blast or two left before the scorching heat of dry season. The sky to the north, where Ishi and his new friend were heading, was growing increasingly dark, and sizzled with lightning. They had just reached the horizon when the first drops of rain began to fall, and then a herd of five bachelors became visible on the banks of a mud-colored river below.

"There they are," spoke the bird, "can you see them, kind host?"

"Of course I can see them. I'm not blind."

Ishi covered the distance to them quickly, having recognized familiar scents from long ago. The herd watched warily as he approached, and then they picked up his scent. Two of them ran out towards him, trumpeting loudly. The egret had to flutter aloft or be crushed as they greeted each other.

Of all the elephants Ishi could have run into, these were the two brothers from the last clan he'd known before being taken from Africa. After Big Black's passing, they had joined him and Little Stream at the annual gathering of the herds and spent most of a season traveling with him. It had been thirty years, but they had somehow all survived. Oh, they would have stories to tell.

They sought shelter under a stand of eucalyptus trees as the rain began pelting down and thunder rumbled in the hills above them. The brothers, Big Feet and Whispers, had stuck together when they left their birth clan because Whispers was virtually a mute; growing up, Big Feet had become his protector and translator, and they were inseparable. They would latch on to bachelor herds from time to time, heeding the old maxim that traveling in numbers increases one's chances of survival. It had certainly worked for them.

They were taken aback when they heard how Ishi had disappeared; they had kept looking for him for several seasons until finally giving up. They were speechless as he told them of the faraway world of the two-leggers; in fact it was so beyond an elephant's comprehension, Ishi had realized many years ago, that he usually spoke of his time there only in vague outlines.

The brothers were approaching their final years as well, and sympathized with Ishi's journey so much that they offered to accompany him the rest of the way. For old time's sake. Ishi was profoundly moved, and accepted their offer on the spot.

Westbrook and the director watched the feed as Werner Brandeis stood behind them. They ascertained that these creatures couldn't have seen each other in over three decades, yet here they were reconnecting as if it had been yesterday. With the proper narration, they explained to their benefactor, the viewing audience would be blown away. Again.

Then the lightning and thunder became too intense for the drone to hang around, and they called it home. What they couldn't see was the egret winging furiously behind it, hissing and clacking, until he finally decided he had chased the thing off, and proudly returned to his host.

That night over dinner, as the rain poured down outside, the stories flew. There was so much history for the Salisbury crew to share with Brandeis, Westbrook and the director that they were all still talking long after midnight. For Brandeis, who was used to giving orders and being deferred to, the company was so different and colorful that he genuinely forgot himself for a while. Westbrook had never experienced this side of the magnate, and actually began to like him.

Russell and Amanda had made quite an impression on Brandeis on their flight down, but now, with several bottles of wine having flowed, they and Kamau regaled the gathering with stories that left him in quiet awe. As they retired for the night he told Westbrook they had to get each of them on camera. They were unforgettable characters—and as much a part of the elephant's story as anything they had.

The next morning the rain had still not stopped, and the Salisbury brain trust realized they might have a problem. The scouts reported back via radio that, yes, there was a problem: the river winding out of Tsavo's southern hills was no longer an easily fordable stream. It was a raging torrent.

Chapter Twenty-Six

Kenya, Crossing Over

THE BACHELOR CLAN STOOD on the banks staring at the river's fury. It had rained for three days and nights since they'd begun traveling together, and the sky was as dark at midday as it was at sundown. No beast, not even an elephant, could cross a river so swollen with runoff. They had reconnoitered the banks for the better part of two days and found no suitable crossing. This meant the end of their journey, at least until the river subsided. And that could be weeks.

The four bulls looked at Ishi, knowing he didn't have that kind of time. All this way…to be stranded one river short of his home? Ishi stared at the fierce, hissing torrent and knew he had to take a chance. Somehow everything else had fallen into place; he had to assume his good fortune would continue.

He had spotted the only feasible crossing about a mile downriver; it was the widest, and therefore the shallowest, section and had a small wooded island about halfway across. If he put in a ways upriver, the current would take him close enough to the island to make landfall, and he could gather his strength there and then make the final push across. He would go it alone—he didn't want the others to risk calamity, since they didn't have a date with destiny like he did.

The brothers didn't like the idea at all. Ishi was not at full strength, they argued, what would he do if he missed the island? He'd end up a waterlogged corpse caught in a thicket of branches and boulders miles downriver. What kind of ending would that be for him? Or for them, who would have to tell the story of his demise to his friends at next season's gathering of the clans?

But Ishi would not be deterred, and when the rain died down to a drizzle he made his way upriver until he found a shallow beach. He said his goodbyes to the brothers, who he hoped to meet when they followed later on—and stepped out into the river.

That night the worldwide audience was riveted by the footage the drone had captured of their hero valiantly attempting to cross the 300-foot wide torrent. They realized soon enough that Ishi was fighting for his life when he went under the first time and didn't come up for fifty yards. No narration or music was needed: virtually everyone watching was on their feet, pleading for him to make it. They didn't realize how much they had invested in this old bull until his possible end was right in front of them, with no one there to rescue him.

The documentary crew was even more distressed. This could be the sudden, totally unexpected end of their beloved hero as well as their show. Brandeis had chosen to let him make the journey on his own, with minimal interference, and now that decision was coming back to haunt them. They realized they had to try to intervene somehow—if that was even possible. Or if it wasn't already too late.

The other bulls ran along the banks shouting encouragement as Ishi churned his legs in the swift, treacherous current. He was making good progress toward the middle when he saw the island coming up fast, and it occurred to him he might miss it. This was life and death, he realized, and he reached down and found another gear to close the gap. He had never dug this deep before, and it might still not be enough. He willed his legs forward with everything he had. Suddenly his feet found the bottom again. He grabbed an exposed tree root just below the surface with his trunk and pulled himself ashore.

He heard his friends trumpeting from the banks, and then saw his egret friend fluttering above him excitedly. He collapsed onto the sand and vomited up water, then felt his trembling legs, pounding heart and aching lungs screaming in protest. This had been even more than he'd bargained for, and he knew he would have to rest overnight to attempt the second half. Two days ago he had seen a set of major rapids about a mile further downriver—what to humans would be considered Class V rapids—and knew that if he didn't make it across in time, that maelstrom would likely be the end of things.

That night as he slept he was visited by an old friend, who spoke to him soothingly and with great affection. Little Streams. In his dream Ishi thought he was actually there with him, but he was in such a deep sleep that he couldn't respond. Little Streams assured him that his time had not yet come, that he would survive this until he completed his journey. Ishi felt overwhelming love and tenderness, and realized with a tinge of sadness that he would be joining Little Streams soon enough.

The next morning he sensed a presence next to him and opened his eyes to a most unexpected surprise. The sun was out, and there was an old friend sitting beside him. The two-legger he had known since his earliest days—the very two-legger who had first found him as an orphan and who had visited him throughout his life. What on earth—was he still dreaming?

When Kamau spoke to him in his familiar voice, Ishi realized it was not a dream. He got to his feet and sniffed his old friend gratefully, and they embraced.

"Ah, my old friend, are you crazy?" asked Kamau. "Do you know what you've got yourself into?"

Ishi was hungry and tired, but Kamau's unexpected presence was a tonic. Ishi looked past him and saw two more dark-skinned two-leggers waiting beside a motorized skiff pulled up onto the island's beach. He recognized their scent—they had been the ones leaving him his grasses; they had been the unseen presences on his journey, and he realized they were like his keepers at the orphanage. Friends.

Then Kamau was pointing to the far shore, and Ishi turned. There stood the two-leggers who, along with Kamau, were one of the main reasons for his journey. Russell and Amanda didn't need to wave or shout for him to pick up their anxiety. They were worried sick, he realized, and had come to offer him encouragement. It was fitting, he mused; they had been there for him at the beginning, and they would be here for him now, at his possible end.

"Are you ready, *tembo?*" asked Kamau as he stroked his head. Ishi met his eyes, and Kamau rapped on his tusks and smiled encouragement. "Then let's go."

With that Kamau walked over to the skiff, pushed it back into the current and jumped in with the two scouts. One of them gunned the outboard, and they came around the head of the little island and waited for him in the current. The drone feed was going viral by now, and almost every channel that was carrying the show was going live.

Ishi gathered his strength and walked to the water's edge. He looked across the river and chose a copse of ghost trees as his guidance point. Then he strode into the current and girded himself with the spirits of his loved ones. He would not perish if he remembered Little Stream's entreaties. He would survive this.

As he stepped off the island's gradual slope, the current tugged at him and he had to lean into it. Then his shoulders slipped under and he fixed his gaze on the ghost trees. Kamau was calling to him encouragingly as the skiff led the way.

Then his head went under. He kept moving his legs forward, his trunk raised above the surface to take in oxygen. When his ears went under he heard an unsettling sound over the whine of the outboard: rocks, big ones, clacking against each other as they tumbled along the bottom.

Then the current became so strong he couldn't keep his feet on the bottom any longer. He lunged upwards and swam, his legs churning with everything he could muster.

Kamau was shouting from the skiff.

"You can do this, Ishi! Come to me!"

Ishi looked up at the shore and realized the ghost trees were no longer in sight. Nor was the beach where his two-legger friends were waiting. He had been swept downriver—how far he couldn't tell, but the distance to the maelstrom had to be closing. He kicked harder, and then he saw Amanda paralleling him on the bank, shouting as she ran.

His lungs were burning; he could barely hear Kamau's entreaties any longer, and the voices in his head were drowned out by his heart pounding in his ears. Suddenly he slammed into something hard and it held him in place, water sucking all around him. A huge boulder, he quickly saw; it was the first of several that were the gates to the maelstrom. His heart sank—and then he saw Kamau next to him leaning out of the skiff.

"Swim to me, *tembo!* You can do this!"

Ishi had never heard panic in Kamau's voice, and it hit him like a bullhook. He knew instinctively that this was the moment he had always recognized in other animals' eyes as they gave up. He had always fought, and he realized he had to fight now, or it was over.

He took a deep breath and launched himself toward the next boulder. He went under momentarily, then came up and kicked furiously, closing on the boulder. He slammed into it and held, the water pinning him to it. He could barely see over the roiling surface, but he knew there was another boulder not far away, and it was almost to the bank and safety. One more. Just one more.

He took a deep breath and lunged.

The audience was so involved in the drama that passersby on streets around the globe could hear shouts and entreaties coming from open windows and wondered what game was being played.

The drones—one close to Ishi, the other offering a wide shot—gave the viewers perspective. The wide shot looked back upriver from above the rapids—more accurately a thundering, several stage waterfall—and everyone could see how close Ishi was to being swept over. The closer drone caught the intensity in Ishi's eyes as he fought, with Kamau's voice shouting to him over the noise of the falls.

No one had ever seen footage like this. There had obviously been countless life and death animal sagas, but nothing in real time, nothing that had viewers so invested in a completely unpredictable outcome. To see such a mighty creature looking so small and helpless in this perilous landscape was more than many viewers could handle, and they had to turn away or cover their eyes.

Ishi's feet slipped on the water-smoothed rocks lining the bottom, and then a large branch slammed into him, sending him under. When he came up he had almost missed the last boulder, and he reached out for it desperately. He got a foothold, barely, and swung himself up onto it.

"You're almost there!" shouted Kamau as the skiff waited just above him, the outboard going full throttle to keep it in place. "Just a little bit more!"

Ishi looked up and saw how close he was to the edge of the maelstrom, and how far down it was to the next level of the river. The realization jolted him and he looked back at the shore with renewed purpose. He lunged toward it and, just as the current started to take him, he felt his feet hit bottom and a little beach came into view. He clambered up the steep bank and willed his deadened legs to cover the last few yards, gasping and wobbling, until he pitched onto the sand.

Kamau was out of the skiff and kneeling beside him.

"You did it, *tembo!* I knew you could do it!" Then Amanda was beside him and she threw her arms around his wet, magnificent head.

Brandeis and Westbrook reached the ridge above them and realized they had been part of the most dramatic, heart-stopping animal footage either of them had ever seen. This phenomenal creature, with these kind people huddled around him on this little beach, were part of an unforgettable climax no matter what happened next. Against long odds, Brandeis' gamble had paid off.

The last leg of the journey was, thankfully, the easiest. Salisbury was half a day's walk away, and after Ishi had been fed and slept for several hours, he raised his sore, aching body to its feet. Kamau and Amanda made the walk with him; Russell was driven behind them in a Jeep. The drones captured their arrival at his "birthplace" just as the sun sank behind the distant hills, the outlines of which Ishi had etched permanently in his memory.

CHAPTER TWENTY-SEVEN

Kenya, The Final Days

Ishi's time at Salisbury was short. He no longer fit in, literally or figuratively. It was an orphanage for the very young, and he was too big to stand in the compound, let alone sleep in his old enclosure. So he slept outside the front gate with Kamau, who rarely left his side. Ishi was beyond exhausted, and he had stopped eating. The river had taken whatever stamina he had left, and in the intervening days it wasn't returning.

After Russell bid a long, emotional farewell to his old friend, Brandeis had Russell and Leslie flown back to London on his jet. Brandeis, Westbrook and the director listened respectfully to Amanda's request that there be no following Ishi if and when he went off to die. They readily agreed; they certainly had enough footage to construct a powerful ending and didn't need to invade his space with drones recording his final moments. If for no other reason, it would be unseemly.

Over dinner that night, Rebecca passed on a story she'd read of how profoundly attached these creatures could become for life. A conservationist named Lawrence Anthony had taken in a wild herd and become their close friend over the years. When he died some years later, the herd made a fifty-mile trek from the bush back to his reserve, arriving three days later to pay their respects. How they knew he had died was a question no one could answer. And the fact that they would come at all—let alone fifty miles—was simply astonishing.

So it was no surprise when various elephants started showing up outside Salisbury to bid their old friend goodbye. The orphans peered through the fence at the sight of these giants as they stood outside telling stories, twining trunks, and bumping and leaning into each other.

Mother Blue was the first to arrive, along with Ishi's mate from her clan, Sad Eyes. Other than Ishi's true mother, Mother Blue had been the most important figure in his life, and he tried in vain to hold back his emotions. But she was a main reason for his journey, and he couldn't contain his tears.

They knew they were all nearing the end of their days, so they caught each other up on the last thirty years of their lives. Mother Blue had the greatest store of wisdom Ishi had ever known, but even she was speechless when she heard the tale of his life. They stood leaning against each other for hours, soaking in each other's life forces.

To Ishi's great surprise, a pair of ancient females showed up that afternoon and shared their memory of him. One night fifty-some years ago they'd come by Salisbury after their clan had heard his cries, and informed him what they'd learned of his birth family's fate. He had been too young— and distraught—to travel with them at the time, so they offered to come by after every rainy season until he was ready. But he had left with Mother Blue's clan soon thereafter and had never run into them again. Now here they were, at the end of rainy season on their same age-old route, marveling at how big and well-loved that little bull had become.

The next day Whispers and Big Feet showed up, having traveled three days downriver until they found a span built by the two-leggers, then hurried all the way to the grand savanna to beseech any elephants who might know of Ishi's fate. When they learned that he had survived they were deliriously happy, but when they were told that he had been escorted by two-leggers, they were agog. Now, as they arrived at Salisbury and stared at the two-leggers lurking everywhere, they were uneasy, to say the least. But Ishi allayed their fears and soon they were dining on the finest grasses an elephant could dream of.

The procession of elephants was duly recorded and sent out to the world as proof of the emotional depth and intelligence of the species. Thanks to Morgan Freeman's sonorous narration, there was not a single doubter (with the exception of the Chinese and the Far East Asians) of the elephant's place in the sentient wild kingdom, right next to dolphins and whales.

On Ishi's third night home, his old friends all departed as if there had been a signal. Kamau checked on him several times as they slept that night, but everything seemed normal. When he awoke just before dawn, Ishi was gone.

He went into Amanda's room with a heavy heart and woke her, and they talked quietly over coffee in the kitchen. It wasn't that they didn't trust Brandeis or Westbrook, but it was their history with Ishi. They both knew these were very likely his last hours. They would keep their next moves to themselves.

Kamau informed her he had a good idea where Ishi might be headed.

My bird friend has rejoined me as I pass through the night to the place that has been calling me. My steps are lighter, and I feel no pain. I am tired, very tired, but I have enough strength left to find my way there.

I have made the journey I promised myself I would. I have seen the friends I needed to see, and I am content. My only regret is leaving my closest two-legger friend behind without waking him to say goodbye, but I know he will understand. I would die defending his life, as I know he would die defending mine. That is the sign of a true friendship in my eyes.

The first hues of dawn began to delineate the landscape around him as he neared his destination, and the night's sounds morphed into the day's. His eyes were getting so cloudy of late that he felt, more than saw, the presence of another bull close by, and then a voice startled him.

"I see you've made it all the way back, my young friend," rumbled Big Black as he sidled up beside him. They were now of equal size, Ishi marveled.

"How did you know where to find me?" asked Ishi.

"Wasn't much of a trick for an old bull." Big Black's skin was wet from head to tail, and a cool mist clung to him like a cloud. This seemed normal in Ishi's current state, so he didn't question it.

"By the way, how did that work out with the ladies?" Big Black continued mordantly. "They take you back into the fold?"

Ishi didn't want to offend him, even now, so he just smiled.

"You were right, of course. I found my way on my own. No need for the ladies."

Ishi never broke stride as he headed for the trees lining a riverine meadow. He noted that the mopane trees were much taller than the last time he'd been here, but the place was still recognizable. The meadow was lush and tranquil, just as it had been fifty years ago.

He realized that Big Black had disappeared from his side, but this didn't disturb him. The bird was still with him, perched between his shoulders.

"You see your kind up ahead?" the egret asked. His eyesight was much better than Ishi's, obviously; Ishi moved forward carefully, afraid to scare off the clan he could now just make out.

"Yes, I see them," he whispered, and there they were, his clan from long ago, grazing quietly on the grasses that grew next to the slow, lazy river. He spotted the outlines of his mother and walked toward her.

There was no need for words as he placed his head against hers; their thoughts were co-mingling as if they were one being. As they held each other's gaze, everything that had ever transpired in his life was communicated in what seemed like a matter of seconds, and Ishi sensed the sadness and pain that only a mother could feel at the tragedies her son had borne. She caressed every inch of his face with her trunk. To Ishi it felt like she had passed inside of him.

And then Ishi saw and felt *her* memories. In a profoundly sad twist, they continued on after the moment of her death, but were comprised of nothing visible, as if she had gone blind. Only emotions, palpable and raw, in an impenetrable darkness. Ishi wept for her, and she for him—and for the life she was never able to lead.

How long they were like this is difficult to say, because time had become elastic. Ishi was well versed with memory and dreams, but this was different. There was certainly nothing to fear, in fact it was actually quite comforting.

Now he felt the rest of his birth family as they surrounded him, each drifting in and out of him with no need for words. Like his mother, they had not aged a day. Their bones were somewhere in the earth beneath where Ishi was now standing, and if their spirits had moved on in the intervening years, they were here now to greet their long-lost son, the lone survivor of their clan. And they were deeply moved to welcome him home.

Ishi looked up and realized his bird friend had flown.

* * *

Kamau shut the Rover off and sat there with Amanda in the stillness, listening to the ticking of the engine as it cooled. He had been to this hillside many times since he'd first visited it fifty years ago and heard the killing down below. Now he would visit the meadow again, quietly and from a distance. It had been twelve hours, and he knew nature would take its course soon after Ishi's last breath. He wanted to say his final goodbye, as well as to remove his tusks so no poachers would defile him. Or profit from him.

Half an hour later he and Amanda reached the meadow on foot and looked for signs of their friend. At first they didn't see anything, and Kamau started to doubt his certainty that this was the spot Ishi would pick. But then Amanda pointed to a dark form that floated in from the sky and lighted in a towering tree. Now they could see dozens of the big birds hidden in the canopy. So he was here, somewhere down below, and the vultures were waiting patiently.

The humans were almost to the river when they saw him. He was lying on his side, as if asleep, and even though they couldn't make out any breathing, or flicking of his tail or trunk, something was keeping the vultures at bay.

Kamau handed Russell's old .375 to Amanda—they were in lion territory, so a warning shot might be necessary—and signaled her to stand watch for him. As he silently approached their friend, it dawned on him that this was exactly the same spot where he had found him fifty years ago. Lying in the same place, but this time with no mother beside him. And like then, showing no sign of life.

He knelt close and studied Ishi's one visible eye, which was closed. Suddenly the eye opened, startling him just like it had startled him fifty years ago.

"Ah, *tembo,* I didn't mean to disturb you," he whispered. "You go back to sleep now."

Ishi slowly raised his trunk to sniff the air and Kamau realized he couldn't see. Kamau signaled Amanda to join him, and they both sat on their haunches watching their old friend as he stared at some place far from here. Then his trunk moved in Amanda's direction—he had picked up her scent. A long, painful expulsion of breath followed, and Amanda fought back tears. She knew that this was exactly what was supposed to be happening, but it didn't make it any easier.

"Ah, my old friend," she whispered. "What I wouldn't give to turn you back into the little calf we once knew… and we could all start over again."

She reached out and stroked him, and then they heard a faint rumble from deep inside him. They lowered their faces to his, breathed in his familiar scent, and kissed his giant, wrinkled cheek through their tears.

Finally Kamau got to his feet and helped Amanda up.

"He knows we are here. Let's give him the time he needs to rejoin his clan."

Amanda nodded, and they slowly withdrew.

* * *

I can see back through time as if it was yesterday. As I said to you at the beginning, all I wanted was to find my home and bid my old friends farewell. I have done that now, and I am free to go.

Whether it is just darkness that I will find, or if it is filled with friends and light, or if it is something I have never considered, I will go to the place all of life before me has gone. We elephants know that. I will either watch over this life from somewhere in the sky, or I will melt into the earth and know nothing but dreamless sleep.

No matter what it is, I am ready.

Epilogue

Every year at the end of rainy season, Kamau visits Ishi's final resting place. He sometimes thinks he feels Ishi's energy passing through him, and after the initial sadness lifts, he smiles for days remembering his old friend.

True to his word, Brandeis funds the orphanage at Salisbury, and whenever he visits Africa he stops in at Salisbury for a night. He has never found more happiness than when they were filming Ishi's journey, and he wants to stay in touch with the marvelous characters he met. But it has never been quite the same.

Three years later Amanda and Leslie laid Russell to rest next to Jean and Terence overlooking Salisbury and Tsavo. Russell had reached ninety, but since he could no longer summon the will or the ability to paint—or even read—he was as ready to go as Ishi had been. What they both found next is obviously the greatest mystery of all.

Amanda watched as her daughters married, moved away, and began starting families, and after three years of living alone accepted Leslie's invitation to take a guest cottage on her estate. On any given day she can choose solitude or a host of interesting friends, and she has begun working on her first novel.

It's called "The Memory of an Elephant."

—Kenya and England, 2015

Made in the USA
Middletown, DE
19 September 2021

48573213R00132